❧The❧ Little Gentleman

By **Philippa Pearce**

Drawings by Tom Pohrt

GREENWILLOW BOOKS
An Imprint of HarperCollins*Publishers*

The text of this book is set in Adobe Garamond.
Book design by Chad W. Beckerman

Library of Congress Cataloging-in-Publication Data

Pearce, Philippa.
The little gentleman / by Philippa Pearce ;
illustrated by Tom Pohrt.
p. cm.
"Greenwillow Books."
Summary: A young girl's dull life is transformed when she meets and befriends an extraordinary talking mole that likes to be read to and tell of his own past exploits throughout the centuries.
ISBN 0-06-073160-5 (trade). ISBN 0-06-073161-3 (lib. bdg.)
[1. Moles (Animals)—Fiction. 2. Friendship—Fiction. 3. Magic—Fiction.] I. Pohrt, Tom, ill. II. Title.
PZ7.P31493Li 2004 [Fic]—dc22 2003067530

First Edition 10 9 8 7 6 5 4 3 2 1

 GREENWILLOW BOOKS

WITH LOVE TO

Sally, Ben, Nat, and Will,

and thanks to Celia for the

naming of Moon

Contents

I

THE LOG AND THE STUMP

OUTSIDE the cottage, lengthways against the wall, lay the ancient ladder with its telltale broken rung; the accident had been some days ago. Inside the house, on his bed, lay Mr. Franklin, with his leg now in plaster, waiting.

He was listening for Mrs. Allum to go: the creak of the front door opening, pause as she got herself out and clicked the door shut behind her. Then the thump of footsteps to the front gate.

He was so impatient that he was already levering himself up to reach his crutches, seriously disturbing his late aunt's white cat, who had been asleep beside him. He hopped to the window and cautiously slid his head around the side to peer out.

His stealthy glance was at once met and held by the gaze of Mrs. Allum's pale, silent, silent-footed granddaughter. He had quite forgotten about this child, whose name he did not even know. He only knew that she turned up regularly with her grandmother for the house-cleaning. He could not guess whether her stare now was hostile, or inquisitive, or just casual.

The child had been there when Mrs. Allum had found Mr. Franklin with a broken leg at the foot of the wrecked ladder. In a great fluster Mrs. Allum had arranged for the ambulance to go to the hospital. Then, while they waited, she had asked her employer why he was climbing ladders at his age, anyway.

He had said evasively, "To get a better view."

Mrs. Allum had said nothing, but sniffed.

After the ambulance, Mrs. Allum had gone back to her cleaning, until Mr. Franklin should be home again from the hospital. He now was, so that, at least, was straightforward. To her, what Mr. Franklin might have been up to was mysterious without being interesting. She had her own work and her own worries.

Now Mr. Franklin ventured another look through the window. Mrs. Allum was easing herself into the driving seat of her old car; the child was inside already.

An anxious moment . . . Then the car started, the gears grumbled, and they were slowly off. Soon they would be at the corner, where the track met the long lane. As always, Mrs. Allum hooted at the corner, although no one could be coming. There was never any traffic, and the nearest house—and distantly at that along the main road—was the Allums' own.

He was by himself at last.

He opened the window wide and leaned out, twisting himself to one side as he did so. In this awkward and uncomfortable position, he could see beyond the track and right across the rough pasture that stretched down to the river, its boundary. He could see the old gray pony grazing and dozing, and there were the trees massed on the higher ground of the further riverbank, and between the pony and the trees, but on the nearer bank—

Yes, just there! There was the great log, once dredged up from the river—the log on which he so often sat, as if on a park bench put on the riverbank for his exclusive use.

There seemed to be nothing else of interest, but he studied this particular view intently.

The late-afternoon sunlight was confusing to his eyes. Without moving from the window, he stretched out an arm and opened a top drawer in his chest of drawers and took out his binoculars. He had bought these, when he first moved into the cottage, to watch the life on the river: moorhen and heron and (if he were ever very lucky) kingfisher.

Now he studied the riverbank around the log for something more, well, out of the ordinary.

No, nothing—unless . . . There seemed to be something like a small stump, probably only a few inches high, just to one side of the log. He had not noticed it before.

He stared at the stump, willing it to be something more than just a stump, imagining from moment to moment that it very slightly moved.

Then, suddenly and unmistakably, it moved.

It had turned slightly. Was it away from the cottage or toward it?

Surely toward it?

"Come *on*!" muttered Mr. Franklin. "Come *on*! What are you waiting for?"

He was so agitated that his trembling fingers missed their hold on the binoculars, and they fell. By the time that he managed his crutches and his plastered leg so that he could scrabble on the floor and get the binoculars to his eyes again, there was no trace of a stump to be seen near the log.

Mr. Franklin stared and stared, although the uselessness of that was plain to him.

At last he twisted himself back from the window into the bedroom and then hopped back to sit on the side of the bed, exhausted. "I shall need help," he said aloud. He was not thinking of the extra cleaning and cooking and washing and washing up that Mrs. Allum was already doing for him in his semi-invalid state. He needed other help of a particular kind.

MRS. ALLUM had had a good many children, and by now several grandchildren. Elizabeth, or Bet, was one. She was the unluckiest, for her mother had been very young at her birth, and her mother and father had split up soon afterward. She had been handed over to her grandparents to bring up. She lived alone with them. Her mother had gone.

This family history was unknown to Mr. Franklin, and anyway, he had felt no interest at all in Bet until now. But here and now he needed someone of her age to help him; she seemed a child surely old enough to be reliable when necessary, yet young enough—this was essential—to have a truly open mind. Another grown man or woman would be of no use to him; he or she would only laugh at his story, think him simply cracked in the head.

He needed the help of someone young enough to credit the possibility of the apparently impossible.

It was some time before the idea of Mrs. Allum's granddaughter floated into Mr. Franklin's mind. He had barely noticed the child before; he did not know her name. She came with her grandmother only after school, at weekends, and during the school holidays.

He had seen her helping her grandmother about the cottage, particularly by reaching to high shelves or squeezing into narrow corners. (Mrs. Allum was short and stout.) He had also sometimes seen the girl dusting his aunt's books and once or twice had caught her peering into them. He had not minded that, as Mrs. Allum had assured him that she was careful.

But did she actually read anything in the books? Or did she open them only from the idlest curiosity, perhaps in the hope of pictures inside?

He set himself to find out this girl's suitability for what needed to be done.

With his plastered leg up on a chair, Mr. Franklin faced the child, who stood beside her grandmother; Mrs. Allum sat. He came to the point at once: "Can you read?"

The girl was startled and—as was her habit—left a silence before her reply. Into this silence Mrs. Allum popped her own answer: "She can. Of course, she can.

So can I, too, even if I'd rather not."

"Read aloud?" asked Mr. Franklin of the child.

"That's easier than reading inside your head," said Mrs. Allum scornfully.

"I wonder if your granddaughter—"

"Bet," said Mrs. Allum. "Bet, short for Elizabeth."

"I wonder if Bet would mind showing me how well she reads aloud. I need someone to do that for me." He added: "Perhaps we could agree on some payment?"

Mrs. Allum waved this aside almost angrily and then said, "You broke your leg, not your glasses, Mr. Franklin."

"I said I needed someone to read aloud *for* me, not *to* me," retorted Mr. Franklin.

Baffled, Mrs. Allum now left the conversation to the other two; she did, however, remain in the room as observer.

Mr. Franklin had a book ready for the test. "A book about worms," he said. "Earthworms. It's not particularly a book for children, so you may find it difficult. Let's start on the first page, from the paragraph beginning 'Earthworms abound in England . . .' But first I want you to read that paragraph over to yourself, inside your head, very carefully. No hurry. Make sure you understand it, or you won't be able to make a listener understand it." He hesitated. "You know what *abound* means?"

"Plenty of 'em," said Bet.

"Right. So read from 'Earthworms abound . . .'" He handed the book over.

To his surprise the girl read aloud not too badly, stumbling only over an unfamiliar word and running out of breath on some of the longer sentences.

Patiently he corrected her pronunciation and pointed out that commas and full stops and colons and semicolons might give a chance to pause, even take a breath. "And this time," he said, "read the whole thing much more slowly, so that any listener can follow the reasoning of it. And read more loudly, too."

She began again more slowly, but he stopped her almost at once. "More loudly, too, remember—much more loudly, especially to begin with."

Now Mrs. Allum protested again. "Mr. Franklin, sir, next thing that girl will be shouting. You're not deaf, Mr. Franklin."

"I said that Bet would be reading aloud *for* me, not *to* me," he repeated.

Mrs. Allum sighed softly.

Bet read the whole long paragraph again and again until Mr. Franklin was as near satisfied as he could hope to be. "Now," he said, "this is all I want you to do. Take the book—carefully, mind—into the pasture. You know where I mean? The old meadow opposite?"

Bet nodded.

"There's a big log there, on its side. You may have

seen me sitting on it, before I broke my leg. Sitting there, reading."

Bet nodded.

"Well, I want you to do the same. Sit there, with a book—this book—and read aloud from it, just as you were doing now. Pay no attention to anybody or to anything that may happen. Just read."

Bet asked, with the book in her hand, "Now?"

"Why not?" Mr. Franklin said. "Yes, now."

Together Mr. Franklin and Mrs. Allum watched Bet as she set off across the pasture, followed some ten paces behind by the white cat. Mr. Franklin clicked his tongue in annoyance. "I should have told her: not the cat."

"What harm can that poor old Moon do?" (Such had been the name given to her cat by the late Miss Franklin.)

Mr. Franklin did not answer.

Meanwhile, crossing the meadow, with nothing but

the book to worry about—and *that* was no worry; she liked books—Bet felt unusually free and happy.

For a child, Bet had to do a good deal of housework. When Mrs. Allum went cleaning in other people's houses, she took Bet with her. "A green girl," she would say, "but another pair of hands." At home, in her grandparents' house, it was the same, and her grandfather, as well, expected to be waited on.

Now she was away from everybody, taking her seat on a log on a riverbank in the sun with a book on her knee. She was supposed to read aloud from the book; her finger was between the pages, at the very paragraph she had been told to read.

She opened the book fully.

Supposed to read . . . Told to read . . .

Suppose she played contrary? Suppose she tricked them, only pretending to read? She could do that.

"I could," she said aloud, but quietly.

What finally decided Bet to read was her own curiosity. She was to read aloud *for* Mr. Franklin, but *to whom?* Not to the cat, Moon, now on the log beside her; he could have been read aloud to indoors at any time. Not to the only other occupant of the meadow, the old gray pony on the farthest side, well out of earshot.

Perhaps the reading would produce the listener.

She began slowly, loudly to read: " 'Earthworms abound in England . . . ' "

As she read, it seemed to her that her reading aloud made a ring of attentive silence around her, which she could even hear in the pauses she made, following Mr. Franklin's instructions. Yet there was nobody there; nothing. Surely—certainly, no listener.

After she had finished, she sat for some time quite still. Then, "Did you like what I read, Moon?" The cat purred, but that was only because Bet had begun to tickle him behind his ear.

The two of them returned to the cottage.

"Nothing?" said Mr. Franklin.

Bet shook her head.

"The cat was an elementary mistake," said Mr. Franklin. "This time we'll keep it shut indoors and you can try again with another piece—a *favorite* piece— from the same book." He had taken the book from her and begun eagerly to turn the pages.

Mrs. Allum said, "Not today, Mr. Franklin, sir. I've him at home waiting for his tea to be got."

"But, surely—" Mr. Franklin pleaded.

"No," said Mrs. Allum. "He don't like to be kept waiting."

"Tomorrow, then," Mr. Franklin said to Bet.

Bet nodded.

As they drove home, Mrs. Allum said: "There weren't nobody in that meadow?"

"No," said Bet.

"Nobody hiding?"

Bet knew that her grandmother was thinking of the trees that, here and there, grew in the meadow: a huge old sycamore, an ash, three horse chestnuts. All had stout trunks behind which it would have been just possible for a child kidnapper to have lurked.

"Nobody," said Bet.

No more was said until they were nearly home. Then Mrs. Allum spoke: "Cracked in the head, poor soul. But no harm in him."

III

THE BOOK AND THE LISTENER

THE next day it rained, in heavy, squally showers.

At school, Bet looked out through the classroom window at the driving rain and thought that at this rate, there would be no visiting the meadow. A pity. The whole project might be crackpot, just as her grandmother had said, but she had liked the meadow, she had liked the book, and she had liked being entrusted with something that Mr. Franklin—even if he were a screw loose—had thought was important. Indeed, she had felt at the time that it really was important.

In the cottage by the meadow, Mr. Franklin hopped about fretfully with the aid of his crutches. He knew that he could rely on Mrs. Allum, of course. She would come, rain or shine, but she would never allow the child to go out in this, even under an umbrella. And then, no doubt, after they'd gone and it was all too late, the weather would clear! Well, then, later, why shouldn't he go into the meadow himself, to the log? But no! He could almost hear Mrs. Allum's voice in protest. It would be madness. The terrain was treacherous for someone on crutches: There was the unexpectedness of all those old, grown-over molehills, and then the tripping grasses. He might fall helplessly, and what then—!

Meanwhile, Mrs. Allum, in mackintosh and plastic hood, was getting on with her household shopping, to which had to be added Mr. Franklin's. She thought of him only to remind herself of what he needed from the shops. And she must remember to collect from him his dirty washing, which she would do at home in her own washing machine.

In the pasture itself, as the rain swept across, the old gray pony took shelter under a tree and turned its rump to the rain. Such weather always passed.

It did, late in the afternoon. The weather had begun to clear just as Mrs Allum prepared to set out with Bet. ("Done your homework, then, girl?" Bet nodded.)

They found Mr. Franklin, his hopes realized after all, in a fever for Bet to venture again into the meadow. From the same book as before he read through with her what he called "the favorite passage." (*Whose* favorite passage? Bet wondered, but never asked.) Again he corrected, explained, advised. Mrs. Allum let them get on with it by themselves. She busied herself in the scullery with Mr. Franklin's washing up. She shut herself in there with Moon, who was not to be allowed into the meadow.

So, this time, Bet set off alone. The afternoon sun shone weakly, hardly warming her; raindrops from the long grass sprinkled her legs and fell into her sandals, but the air smelled fresh and sweet after the rain. A heron rose from the river ahead of her and sailed aloft on huge, leisurely wings. Her spirits rose and sailed with the bird. She did not hurry. She simply strolled toward the log as though the rest of the day belonged to her, alone and free.

She held the book high against her chest, in case it might be dampened by a stray raindrop. She remembered Mr. Franklin's explanations and advice on this further reading. She must be prepared for some odd words. "A Volunteer," he had told her, meant a particular kind of soldier. Then, "the Peewit" was a bird—and she needn't bother about its other name, in Latin. "You can skip the Latin," Mr. Franklin had said. (But she rather liked the idea of another name in another language.)

Bet reached the log and sat down. Again, she was unhurried, enjoying herself. She opened the book at last and lowered her eyes to it and began reading once again about earthworms.

"It has often been said," she read, slowly, loudly, "that if the ground is beaten or otherwise made to tremble, worms believe that they are pursued by a mole and leave their burrows." (Out of the corner of her eye, Bet was aware of something like a movement in the rank grass at one end of the log; but she read steadily on.) "From one account that I have received, I have no doubt that this is often the case," (The movement in the grass had subsided.) "but a gentleman informs me that he lately saw eight or ten worms leave their burrows and crawl about the grass on some boggy land on which two men had just trampled while setting a trap; and this occurred in a part of Ireland where there were no moles. I have been assured by a Volunteer that he has often seen many large earthworms crawling quickly about the grass, a few minutes after his company had fired a volley with blank cartridges. The Peewit—" (Bet took a breath to tackle the Latin and managed not too badly.) "The Peewit (*Tringa vanellus*) seems to know instinctively that worms will emerge if the ground is made to tremble; for Bishop Stanley states (as I hear from Mr. Moorhouse) that a young Peewit kept in confinement used to stand on one leg and beat the turf with the other leg until the worms crawled out of their burrows, when they were instantly devoured. Nevertheless, worms do not invariably leave their burrows when the ground is made to tremble, as I know by having beaten it with a spade, but perhaps it was beaten too violently."

Bet had reached the end of the prescribed paragraph.

Without shutting the book she looked downward to the grass tussocks where she thought she had seen movement earlier.

And there it was.

A very small, compact animal, probably less than a handspan in length and almost completely covered in close-growing, glossy black fur. Only the extreme tip of its muzzle—its nose—was exposed in a faintly glistening, dusky pink. It seemed to have no eyes, no ears. It leaned out of its hole, hunched shoulders and neck and head all in one, as someone might lean from an open window, settling down on the windowsill for a gossip with a neighbor. So Bet thought bemusedly, but then she saw that instead of resting on folded arms, the creature faced her with large hands splayed outward on either side. The fingernails were not exactly claws but were long and very strong-looking and also earth stained.

The mole spoke as if indeed in mid-flow of neighborly

chat: " . . . And you probably have little idea of how delicious—how toothsome—how *scrumptious*—they are when eaten fresh. Of course, I have my worm larder—" He corrected himself. "Worm larders, well stocked, but the earthworm pursued, or promptly pounced upon, and eaten fresh—as I've said—Ah! the earthworm, there's nothing like it! You can have your slugs and your wireworms and your leatherjackets and as many ground beetles as you like to eat—snap! crackle! crunch! You can have them all! There's nothing to equal the near liquefaction of worm meat as I pass its length through my fingers, sieving out the earth granules from the creature's incessant feeding. Or alternatively tear it to eat at once in great guzzling, gulping chunks."

He paused. "You don't say much, do you?"

Bet, dazed, said nothing.

The mole continued. "Very unlike Franklin. I suppose he's dead?"

"No," said Bet. "No."

"Pity," said the mole. "Anyhow, he will die. They all do. You will, in due course." He sighed, then brisked up again. "Meanwhile, you read well. You can come again."

Bet said, "Mr. Franklin broke his leg, but my gran says he'll be able to walk out and about again quite soon."

Up to now the mole's voice had been small but clear and very exact; now it suddenly rose into a ragged squeal. "You can tell Franklin that he is *never* to come to me again, and certainly I have no intention of visiting *him*, as he has suggested. I distrust and dislike the man. He spoke to me—to *me*—of a vivarium. He has a mind vicious and ignoble."

Bet stared at the enraged mole.

"Now read on."

Bet did as she was told.

Later, on her way back over the meadow, Bet pondered. She knew the word *noble*, of course, but not ig*noble*. Paired with *vicious*, it sounded bad—what her grandmother would call "real nasty." This was what the mole thought of Mr. Franklin. And all because of something called a vivarium.

When she reached the cottage, "Well?" Mr. Franklin asked. "A truly astonishing experience, eh?" Bet nodded. "Unbelievable, wouldn't you say? Go on—tell me—tell me!" But in fact, Mr. Franklin was far too excited to be told anything by Bet or anybody else. Instead, he was telling of his own experience in the meadow, of how one day this extraordinary mole had appeared at his feet as he sat on the log and asked to be read to. "But no, no— before that, we got into conversation, and I discovered how—in spite of his command of speech—how very ignorant he was. Even of the natural world about him and its history. He asked me to read to him, and I was going to suggest something that would be really illuminating, educative—"

Mr. Franklin suddenly remembered he was talking to a

child. "Something—well, useful to him, and up-to-date, of course. But oddly, he'd got hold of this one big name from the past—of course, very important indeed, absolutely so, but all the same, of the past . . . You've probably never heard of Charles Darwin?"

"At school I have," said Bet. "He was in the reign of Queen Victoria. A scientist. Evolution."

"Very roughly, yes," said Mr. Franklin. "A truly great man, with his theory of the Origin of Species by Means of Natural Selection. So I was going to read that book *The Origin of Species* to this extraordinary mole—at his own request, mind—but I happened to mention that Charles Darwin had also written a book on earth-worms, and do you know"—Mr. Franklin began to laugh wildly—"this mole phenomenon insisted I should get hold of *that* book by Darwin and read it to him. And can you guess why? Because the glutton loves his food, and the food he loves best are earthworms!"

Mr. Franklin steadied himself; he summed up: "Our mole has a shallow, frivolous, and uninquiring mind."

As she listened to Mr. Franklin, Bet remembered that she had to tell him, from the mole himself, that he was not to come again—was never to come again—to read on the log in the meadow. Should she tell him that now or later? It would be difficult now, but it might become even more difficult later.

She decided: now.

And told him.

Mr. Franklin was bewildered, then outraged. "Not go to him in the meadow when my leg is right again? Whyever not?"

"He didn't like something you talked about." The word the mole used had been strange to her; she had no idea what it meant. All the more important that she should get it exactly right now: the mole's word, Mr. Franklin's word. "You talked to him about a viv—a vivarium."

Carefully she repeated the word and then watched a red flush begin to creep over Mr. Franklin's face. She could not tell whether it was a sign of anger or, perhaps, of shame. Mr. Franklin seemed about to speak but did not.

Into this silence walked Mrs. Allum with her bag crammed full of Mr. Franklin's dirty washing for her machine. "Time to be off," she said to Bet.

They went off together as usual, leaving Mr. Franklin alone with his thoughts.

IV

GO-BETWEEN

MRS. ALLUM had said that Mr. Franklin was "on the mend." The hospital agreed. After a few weeks the plaster was taken off his damaged leg, and he was given two walking sticks to use, instead of crutches. Then one walking stick, with which he hobbled about the cottage and even into its little garden.

But never into the meadow.

Whatever deep disagreement there had been between himself and the mole was not referred to again.

Meanwhile Bet went to and fro between the mole in the meadow and Mr. Franklin in the cottage with news of whatever of interest was said or told—or asked for.

After Darwin on earthworms, the mole asked for poetry by Tennyson. He had always enjoyed, he said, the poems of Lord Tennyson when they were read to him by a Miss X. (So he referred to her.)

"Miss X?" said Mr. Franklin sharply when Bet reported this. "Who's she? Where does she live? Find out all about her for me, Bet. She will be another source of information on this mole phenomenon."

But the mole was secretive, even with Bet, and simply repeated his request for the poetry of Tennyson.

Annoyed, Mr. Franklin asked Bet: "And does your friend with a taste for Tennyson ever say, 'Please'?"

Bet thought for a moment. "No."

"Then you can go back to him and remind him that he is asking a favor of a civilized human being," said Mr. Franklin, not letting go from his hands his aunt's copy of *The Complete Poetic Works of Alfred Lord Tennyson in One Volume.*

Bet reported back to the mole this refusal, using Mr. Franklin's own words, rather curious to see what the mole would think of them. He gave a small-sized but very disagreeable guffaw. "Civilized, indeed! I could tell you of barbarities—brutalities—committed by so-called civilized human beings not just on my mole species but on other human beings. However, I won't speak of that, for it would turn your stomach. Meanwhile, to this self-styled 'civilized' gentleman, I say now, *Please*, can we borrow your Tennyson?"

The book was lent, and Bet began reading from it. The mole remembered favorite poems, which Bet had to find. Quite early in the readings, the mole asked for a poem beginning

On either side the river lie
Long fields of barley and of rye . . .

"That's 'The Lady of Shalott'!" Bet exclaimed with pleasure. Her class at school had read the poem and acted the story. Bet had been given only a very small part in the acting. "A burgher," she explained to the mole, adding as a joke: "Not the kind of burger you eat. My burgher was a citizen of Camelot."

Either the joke did not appeal to the mole, or he did not know about beefburgers. He just said, "Oh?"

Bet read "The Lady of Shalott" several times, each time liking it better and reading it better. The mole

complimented her on her reading and, rather hesi-
tantly, had a suggestion to make. "We are not always
safe from strangers in this meadow. We need a word
warning—a Beware!—which you can give to me
secretly when there is an intruder. Here we are by a
river, just as was Sir Lancelot." The mole quoted from
the poem:

"Tirra-lirra," by the river
Sang Sir Lancelot.

"Suppose you sing out 'Tirra-lirra!' to me when you
see any danger? Then I shall know not to appear aboveground."

They agreed upon this useful arrangement.

From time to time people did visit the meadow.
Every so often someone would come to check that the
old gray pony was all right—as he should be in summer,

with grass to eat and the river to drink from. Less often came a man with a ride-on grass cutter. Before he began the mowing, he spent some time kicking flat the more recent molehills, which would otherwise obstruct his machine and throw grit into its works. "That'll teach the little black vermin!" he muttered every time he did so.

The mole overheard and was sourly amused. When the man and his machine were gone, he explained to Bet: "Ignorant people suppose they can harm a mole by destroying the molehills he raises. But the hills are just heaps of waste earth from tunnelings below. It doesn't matter what happens to them. If you were a sensible size—small enough, I mean—I could take you under-ground, and then you would understand how the whole tunneling system works."

Bet had given a gasp, which perhaps the mole noticed. "But oh! couldn't you possibly . . . *somehow*—"

She left her question hanging in the air.

"No!" said the mole. "I'm not a magician. No!"

This was a conversation which Bet reported back to Mr. Franklin only in part. He thought the "Tirra-lirra" watchword sounded silly, and she did not repeat to him the mole's "If you were small enough . . . " Anyway, Mr. Franklin was much more interested in the possibility of tracking down the mole's Miss X and finding out all she knew. "And do you think, Bet, there's anyone else who's read to him?" he asked.

Bet hesitated. "There was a boy who talked with him a lot and read *Just William* stories that made him laugh. But he grew up and went off to fight in a war."

"A war? Which war? There are wars all over the globe nowadays. Surely the young man said where he'd been, when he came back?"

"He didn't come back," said Bet.

"Oh," said Mr. Franklin. Then: "This mole seems to

have been fitting a lot of conversation and being read to into a very short life."

Bet gazed at Mr. Franklin doubtfully.

He asked, "What have I said that you're staring at me so?"

"Nothing," said Bet. "Sorry." Her grandmother had always told her she must not stare at other people whatever silly things they might say. One must keep one's thoughts to oneself.

V

MRS. ALLUM STANDS TO REASON

M R. FRANKLIN had discussed with Bet the like-
lihood that his aunt had been one of the mole's
readers. It seemed such an obvious thing. In a round-
about way he questioned Mrs. Allum. When his aunt
had gone into the meadow, had she usually taken a

book with her? Was there already a log there, and did she settle down on it to read?

"Your auntie never went into that meadow at all," said Mrs. Allum. "She never would. Never."

Mr. Franklin was taken aback. "Why not?"

"Your auntie was poorly every spring and summer with the hay fever, wasn't she? Streaming nose, streaming eyes, headaches—oh, she suffered! So the last place she'd go into was a meadow." Mrs. Allum paused, then decided to add to what she had said. "I can tell you who did go there."

"Who?"

"Moon. In your auntie's time here, he was a young cat. A great hunter. He went often into the meadow— fairly haunted it. Never came back with a moorhen or even a mouse, but he was hunting *something*."

Moon was much older now, but Bet suspected that he was still interested. Regularly, however, when she went out to the log, Moon was shut away into the cottage with

Mrs. Allum, in kitchen or scullery or in whichever room where she happened to be working.

Arrangements are seldom perfect.

One day, when Bet was halfway across the meadow, she heard from the cottage behind her sounds of consternation and calling. Somebody—Mr. Franklin or her grandmother—was shouting her name, and even as Bet paused to look back and listen, a white shape shot past her: Moon, leaping lightly and very fast and going in the same direction—toward the log.

Startled, Bet looked at once to the log and now could see grassy topsoil heaving up into a ridge. The mole, uneasy at using always the same exit hole, had decided to approach the log this time by a surface tunnel, only a few inches deep. Bet could see earth heaving and crumbling, and so, apparently, could Moon. The cat was by now only a few feet away from whatever was happening. He dropped down into a crouch, absolutely attentive, every muscle ready for the pounce when the ridge maker should emerge.

"Tirra-lirra!" screamed Bet, at a pitch and in a style quite unlike anything the bold Sir Lancelot might have used. The mole heard. For a split second his tunneling froze. Then it resumed, but steeply and frantically downward.

And Moon?

The cat, at Bet's wild cry, missed his pounce—and was also instantly aware of the danger behind him. Indeed, Bet had heaved up in both hands over her head *The Complete Poetic Works of Alfred Lord Tennyson* and now hurled it overarm in the direction of Moon with a force that she had never imagined that she possessed and then toppled facedown among the plantains and daisies. She hardly had time to realize the mole's dive underground into safety.

If *Lord Tennyson* had reached Moon, the weight

could have flattened him, or at least winded him, but the book fell short, with a thud. The cat had sprung forward into a swift zigzag, stopping only at a safe distance to look back at the girl and what she had thrown, both grounded now, yards apart, harmless. He sat down and began—perhaps a little shakily—to groom himself.

From the cottage Mr. Franklin and Mrs. Allum had heard Bet's scream and seen her pitch violently forward with the force of her own hurling. They hurried from the cottage as fast as Mrs. Allum's stoutness and Mr. Franklin's lameness would allow. Mrs. Allum, ahead, tried to open the meadow gate, failed, and at once—to Mr. Franklin's amazement—began to climb it. In this, surprisingly, she was not unskillful, but after all, Mr. Franklin realized, she had once been a young woman; before that, a girl. When she reached the top, she simply fell off, down into the meadow, then picked herself up again and blundered on toward Bet, already crying out to her, "You all right, girl? Oh, how's my girl then!" She seemed a ridiculous figure, and yet Mr. Franklin did not feel like laughing.

Mrs. Allum reached her granddaughter, knelt by her, spoke to her, coaxed her to sit up, stand up. Then she fetched the *Tennyson* from where it lay and, carrying it, led Bet back to the meadow gate. Mr. Franklin had had time to get the gate open and followed them into the cottage.

In the past Mrs. Allum had always refused to break off her work to take even a quick cup of tea. Today Mr. Franklin insisted on tea for all of them, with milk and with plenty of sugar "against the shock we've all had." He also felt that the time had come for Mrs. Allum to have some explanation of what had been going on in the meadow.

He began by explaining that there was a mole who surfaced when Bet sat on the log.

"I knew *that*," said Mrs. Allum. "I've good eyes in

my head; I don't need a spyglass." This was a reference to Mr. Franklin's binoculars.

Mr. Franklin proceeded with his explanations. This mole was an exceptional—an amazingly unusual—specimen. It had language; it liked to be read to, and to talk.

Mrs. Allum listened without interruption to what Mr. Franklin had to say. Only when she was sure he had quite finished, did she speak. "A mole—yes. A mole that's half tame—yes. But a mole that listens and talks—no. That's the fancy that you have between you." (She was including Bet with Mr. Franklin in what she said.) "Bet's only a child still and has childish fancies. And you, Mr. Franklin, sir—I remember your auntie saying you were a great reader of books." Mrs. Allum shook her head in deep regret. "Reading like that isn't good for the brain. Tires it *and* overexcites it." She sighed. "You mean no harm, Mr. Franklin, but what you've told me don't make sense. Fairy-tale stuff. It can't happen, so it hasn't happened." She stacked the cups and saucers for the washing up and now heaved herself to her feet to deliver her final judgment: "Stands to reason."

Mrs. Allum left them for the scullery. When they were alone together, facing each other over what had been the tea table, Mr. Franklin said, "Well, I didn't get very far with your grandmother on that subject."

"No," said Bet.

He said, "You know, Bet, you acted with great presence of mind just now, in the meadow. You saved the mole's life."

"No," said Bet.

"Nonsense!" said Mr. Franklin. "Don't be modest. That cat would have caught the mole and killed him."

"He'd have caught him," Bet agreed wearily, "he might have hurt him badly, but I'm almost sure he couldn't have killed him. Because, I think . . . " She sighed; it was too difficult a thing to explain just now. Her voice trailed away.

Mr. Franklin said gently: "We won't argue, Bet. But what's clear is that a mole, like any other wild animal, is always at risk of sudden death. Moreover, the natural life of a mole is, anyway, comparatively short. Five years, at the most." Bet opened her mouth as if to start some objection, and Mr. Franklin raised his voice a little. "Believe me, that's what all the books say, and I've made a point of reading the subject up. I get specialist books from London, you know. Only five years' life span. And already the mole is not a young mole; one can assume that. Would it not be a wonderful thing for him if he could spend his last years in safety and in comfort?"

Bet did not answer, just waited.

Mr. Franklin shifted a little in his chair and cleared his throat. He said, "In the garden of this cottage there is room for me to construct a first-rate vivarium."

Here was that word again. Bet waited.

"A vivarium," Mr. Franklin repeated carefully. "It

would be something I myself would build to be the mole's home, in every possible way like the place where he lives at present. Without the deadly risks that he runs now."

He paused.

Bet said nothing.

Mr. Franklin gained confidence. "Imagine, Bet, a mole with his own ready-made nesting box for sleeping, which is connected with wire mesh tubing of the right size and in every other way made as nearly as possible to resemble the mole's own familiar earth tunnels. This tubing tunnel leads to a really spacious box of good earth, which I shall be frequently renewing and which I shall be supplying regularly with fresh earthworms and whatever other foods a mole might fancy." On the wings of his enthusiasm, Mr. Franklin forgot to be careful. "Don't you think, Bet, that's an ideal habitat for a mole in captivity?"

"In *captivity?*" repeated Bet.

Too late. Mr. Franklin wished he had not used the word and tried to cover his mistake. "Really, it would simply be what people call a safe house, Bet. And there I shall be able to watch the mole, to listen to him, to talk to him, to *study* him. That's the point, to study him, to understand him and his amazing abilities, while he is in the safety of his very own home."

"In captivity . . . " said Bet.

"But safe and comfortable for the last year or so of his short life," said Mr. Franklin. "Don't you see, Bet? Don't you think that my plan is helpful and humane?"

"No," said Bet. "No, I think it's ig-ignoble."

Abruptly she rose from the table.

"Wait!" Mr. Franklin pleaded.

In vain.

Bet left him to find her grandmother elsewhere in the cottage. She preferred her company and her silences.

VI

MUD AND BLOOD

ONE word—*vivarium*—lay between Mr. Franklin on one side and Bet and the mole on the other. It was an enemy frontier, manned. Nowadays Bet viewed Mr. Franklin with sharp suspicion, the selfsame suspicion felt by the mole.

On his side, Mr. Franklin might have given up his idea of a mole vivarium, but he could not give up his wanting—his longing—to know more about this extraordinary mole: to know him through and through. This was a thirst for knowledge and understanding from which—in quite different circumstances—he had suffered many times during his life. When his aunt died and left him this remote, rather tumbledown cottage, he had jumped at the chance of solitude and quiet. Here he could assemble his ideas, sort them and arrange them, perhaps even begin writing the book he was always thinking about. It was to be the kind of book that explained *everything* in nature. A very big book, indeed! The trouble was that Mr. Franklin could never quite decide where to begin.

Meanwhile, he had to rely on Bet for any further light to be thrown on the nature of the mole, who in himself seemed to break the laws of nature.

And now the time had come for Bet's school to take its half term holiday. For several fine days Bet was away from home in a school party at a field study center. ("And why she needs to go away to a field to study when she's surrounded by 'em, I don't know," grumbled her grandmother, but she paid up for the trip, all the same.) During this short period Mrs. Allum still came to the cottage, of course, but without Bet. Moon was allowed freely into the meadow, if he wished, but he seemed to have lost interest.

In Bet's absence Mr. Franklin determined to attempt once more what Bet would have been doing, what he had been forbidden to do. He hobbled out to the log with a book to read aloud: Darwin's *The Origin of Species*. He had marked an interesting page about the so-called blindness of moles, which he thought might tempt the mole out to listen.

He sat on the log in the hot sunshine; he waited a

little, hoping that his footsteps had been heard below-ground—but knowing that their irregularity might have warned the mole that this was the visitor he did not want. He began to read slowly, clearly, and, above all, loudly, in a deliberately "listen to this" kind of way. But nobody seemed to want to listen; nobody appeared.

He finished his reading, waited again, without much hope, and then went back to the cottage. Mrs. Allum had watched him and heard his voice carrying across the meadow. She said, "None so deaf as them as don't want to hear." Then, to console him: "That little old mole, he's still there. He'll pop out right enough when my girl gets back."

Mrs. Allum was wrong. When Bet came back to the log after her half term break, there still seemed to be no mole. At least, as far as Mr. Franklin could see with his binoculars. On the first day of her return, Bet was on the log, reading—but reading only for a very short while. Then she set the book aside and stooped almost to the ground at the spot where the mole should have appeared. Was she looking for him or calling to him?

After a time Bet stood up. She left the log altogether, to roam the meadow—but not quite aimlessly. She came to the riverbank and walked slowly along it until she reached a point where she stopped. She remained there, standing still, looking either at the river or across it to the trees on the rising ground beyond; her back was to the cottage.

From the cottage Mr. Franklin was struck by the stillness of the figure on the riverbank. He began to feel uneasy, even alarmed. He went out to the field gate and called across the meadow. "Bet, are you all right?" There was no answer; no movement.

In the end, he set off across the meadow and had almost reached the riverbank when Bet turned. She faced him. To his dismay, he saw that her whole face was awash with tears that still poured from her eyes. He had never seen her cry before; he had never imagined that she could cry like this: Bet Allum, the silent, secret child.

He could only ask, "What is it?"

"Oh!" she wailed, and then thickly through her tears: "The mole—the mole has killed the heron!"

"I'm so sorry—so very sorry," he said, as indeed, he felt that he was. But Mr. Franklin had once been a schoolmaster, and now, in his teacherly way wanting to get things right, he added: "You mean, of course, that the heron has killed the mole."

"No!" said Bet. She gestured toward the river. Mr. Franklin took a step forward to look down at the water. At first all he saw was the river and the river weeds that, in midstream, had gathered themselves into a kind of floating island. But not an island—no, the body of a great bird, half submerged in water and river weed, dead, its gray and white feathers filthied with mud and the remains of blood. As it turned a little with the turning of an eddy, he could see the fatal wound, a ragged gashing just at the base of the long neck, almost in the breast and at the heart itself.

"Some brute of a man with a gun," said Mr. Franklin.

"No," said Bet. "The mole. It was so hot that he went down to the river, and the heron was there—" She began to cry again as she remembered what the mole, himself still bloodied and exhausted, had so recently told her. Gradually Mr. Franklin understood the story retold between her sobs. The heron had been in wait for fish, had seen the mole instead, caught him and swallowed him, whole and alive. The mole had gone down the bird's long throat, clawing and biting at the inner walls of the gullet, fighting frantically for his life. And in the end— "He didn't mean to kill the heron," sobbed Bet, "but it was the only way out." Mr. Franklin, staring at the dead bird, saw that what Bet had just said was literally true. The dreadful wound had been made *from the inside*, not by any bullet or other attack from the outside. The mole had fought his way out from inside the heron's body; the heron had died of internal injuries.

"I want to bury it," said Bet. "Properly. In this meadow. By this river."

"No," said Mr. Franklin. "That's simply not possible, Bet. And not necessary, anyway. Look, it's moving all the time a little with the current, and when the weather breaks, as will happen anytime, the first flush of rain will carry it downstream and underwater. Then the fishes and all the other hungry little river creatures—"

Bet put her hands up to her face in a kind of resignation.

Mr. Franklin said, "These things happen," and then felt how stupid, how *poor* that was as a saying of comfort.

They began walking back together. When they reached the log, Bet said, "Will you take the book back indoors for me? Please."

Mr. Franklin left her sitting on the log but already stooping down toward the mole hole.

Mrs. Allum greeted him: "What were that about, then?"

"The heron. It's dead."

"Well, there!" said Mrs. Allum. "A fine bird like that. I did like to see it." She sighed. Then: "Well, there's living, and then there's dying. For all of us."

She went back to her cleaning. Mr. Franklin pondered what she had said. It didn't really amount to much more than he had said to the grief-stricken child on the riverbank, and yet it was much better.

Through his binoculars he watched Bet, still in the meadow. She was no longer sitting on the log, but kneeling beside it. The mole had dragged himself partly out of his hole, and Bet was touching him here and there with careful fingers. She would be picking at the clottings of mud and blood in his fur and also gently rubbing away at the ache of his muscles. Mr. Franklin also thought that she was perhaps singing, although at this distance he could catch no sound.

Meantime, as Mr. Franklin had predicted, heavy clouds had begun to gather; big drops of rain fell. Mr. Franklin saw the mole withdraw into his tunnel, and Bet came slowly, heavily back to the cottage. As soon as she arrived, he said, "Bet, I must tell you that I have changed my mind. I have given up the idea of a vivarium. Utterly." Bet nodded. "All the same," he added wistfully, "I'd still like to know more. About Miss X, in particular. A firsthand source, you know."

Bet nodded. "Perhaps . . . " She sat down on the nearest chair and closed her eyes. Her face, usually pale, was white with tiredness; she wanted only to go home.

Mr. Franklin saw that he must be content with that "Perhaps . . . " He tiptoed away.

VII

TRUST

THE death of the heron made a difference in the acquaintanceship of Bet and the mole. A day or two afterward Mr. Franklin, looking out over the meadow, saw that Bet was sitting on the ground with her back against the log, instead of sitting on it. The book remained on the log, closed. The mole, as usual, was hunched in the mouth of his tunnel. They were deep in talk.

Then Bet deliberately stretched herself out on the grass, so that her head was on a level with the mole. At the same time she extended one arm so that the fingers of her hand, palm upward, almost touched him, half in, half out of his tunnel mouth.

The mole crept forward onto the human hand, so that the black velvety length of him reached from Bet's fingertips to the beginning of her wrist. He settled there, and the fingers and the hand and the arm never moved.

The sun shone warmly down upon them both.

The mole said, "I trust you as I have trusted few before. Only Miss X; only Master Y. Do you know that?"

"Yes," said Bet. "I do."

"On one occasion you saved me from attack and

injury; on a second you cared for me when I was in severe distress." (Bet noticed that he didn't speak of escaping death itself.) "Moreover," he continued, "you have always behaved toward me without any air of presumed superiority: You have not condescended; you have not patronized. We have always spoken together freely and equally, as mammal to mammal."

He paused. Bet understood that she was being praised, as well as thanked. She knew the honor of it. She did not know what properly to say in reply; it seemed best to say nothing.

"You must know," said the mole, "that during my travels there were others, besides Miss X and Master Y, to whom I made myself known. Each one, I soon discovered, would have betrayed me, usually to make a raree-show of me—to exhibit me publicly for money. Such people were despicable. I fled them. Even your Mr. Franklin would have made me his prisoner—"

"No! No!" Bet interrupted anxiously. "I was going to tell you: He's given up the idea of a vivarium. He really has. Really."

The mole tipped his head heavenward in a way that suggested some degree of disbelief. But all he said was: "He has a vivarium mind."

Bet felt that they should be fair to Mr. Franklin. She said, "He only wants to *know*, to *understand*. That's all."

"All!" said the mole.

A silence settled between them.

Bet was thinking of what Mr. Franklin, knowledge-hungry, had said of Miss X. "On the entire mole phenomenon," he had declared, "Miss X could be—almost certainly is—a mine of information. I *must* speak with her."

Bet sighed.

"Difficult," the mole agreed. (He seemed to have no problem with following a train of thought inside Bet's own head.) "Perhaps best to tell him the truth about Miss X—the whole truth about everything. It will, I fear, be a great shock. So be careful how you go about it. At first, inform him indirectly. Encourage him to infer the true state of affairs for himself."

Bet thought for a moment. Then: "I could tell him what you once told me about the fire in the church porch."

"A useful start," said the mole. "Surely that should give him some inkling."

"And then there's Miss X and her white cockatoo. The naming of the cockatoo."

"Aha!" said the mole. "Clever, very clever! And conclusive. Excellent."

Now that they had made a plan, they could relax, reclining in the sunshine and talking of this and that. There were many easy, drifting pauses. Bet was thinking back to the earlier part of their conversation, when the mole had spoken of trusting Miss X and Master Y and now herself. She wondered if she dared . . . Why not? So she nerved herself to ask her question. Abruptly she said, "And I can trust you, too, please, can't I?"

The mole was surprised. "Of course. Trust, at its best, is mutual."

Bet was now silent, but only because she was struggling with the words to say more.

The mole encouraged her. "Trust me then. Tell me."

"It's my mother," said Bet. "When I was born, she ran away and left me with my granny and my grandpa. I've never seen her since. No one has. And now my gran has had a letter from her."

"A letter?"

"She says she's married now, with a proper husband and they have a baby, a little boy. They want me to go and live with them, so that we can be one family together."

"Family life," the mole said thoughtfully. "I know

of family life from Miss X and Master Y, but their situations were quite unlike what you have just described."

Bet said, "They live somewhere called Disham. It's a town quite a way off. I'm supposed to be going there with my gran, just for the day. To meet my mother. We're going quite soon. Saturday week. But I'm not sure I want to go. I'm not sure I want to meet my mother. I'm not sure I want to live with a strange family. And I'm not sure I want to leave my gran. Oh, I'm not sure about *anything*!"

"Come!" said the mole. "Calm yourself, child. One step at a time, as Miss X used to tell me." He thought. "Yes, and I think Miss X would have said that you *must* meet your mother before you can possibly know what you really feel about her. Isn't that so?"

"But I keep wondering what she may be like. I keep wondering and I keep thinking—"

"Miss X always told me that bridges should not be

crossed before one came to them As for wondering and worrying about the future, she said that one should occupy one's mind with the present and do one's duty."

"Duty?" Bet puzzled over the word. "You mean, tell Mr. Franklin the whole truth?"

"Well, that is what we agreed, and I think Miss X would have thought that proper."

Again Bet pondered. Then: "Yes, I'll do that. Thank you."

So once more they returned to their former pleasant, idle style of conversation.

Then the mole seemed to lose interest in what he himself was saying. In spite of the heat of the sun, he began to shiver. Bet could feel the shaking of his body through the skin of the palm of her hand, where he still lay.

"What is it?" she asked.

He could answer only with difficulty, in gasps of speech. "This is unnatural . . . to me . . . as mole. I am unused to this . . . to this prolonged exposure . . . to sun . . . to outer air. If you will excuse me . . . cannot stay . . . "

Backward he was already shuffling off her hand and into the welcoming darkness of the tunnel mouth behind him.

She called after him, "Good-bye!"

From the depth of darkness his voice came back to her suddenly strong and cheerful again: "*Au revoir*! And good luck!"

VIII

SHOCK

NEXT day in the cottage, Bet faced Mr. Franklin across the kitchen table. As she and the mole had agreed, she was talking freely about Miss X.

"And the mole could give you Miss X's address?" Mr. Franklin asked eagerly.

"No, but he said her father was a vicar, and—"

"A vicar! Where?"

"I don't know. Somewhere in England. It doesn't matter."

"Of course, it matters, Bet! For tracing her whereabouts."

Bet had hurried to begin the little speech that she had prepared. "Miss X had younger brothers who went to the university. One of them brought her *The Origin of Species*—you know, the book Charles Darwin wrote."

"Of course, I know. But what has that to do with anything?"

"Miss X began reading it to the mole. The vicar—her father—never knew about the mole, but he found the book."

"Well?"

"He burned it the next Sunday morning. In the church porch."

Mr. Franklin was flabbergasted. "What an extraordinary thing to do in this day and age!"

"Yes." Bet was pleased at the effect her words had had. Surely now Mr. Franklin must have some *inkling*. If only, from what she had told him, he would begin to *infer* . . .

Then Bet made her mistake. "Now I'll tell you about the cockatoo that Miss X was given as a little girl. The mole said she was always very fond of birds and animals—"

" '*Was* fond'? You're now speaking of Miss X in the past?"

"Yes, well—"

"Then has Miss X died?"

"Yes, but really—"

"Miss X has died! I've just missed my firsthand witness!"

"It's not like that at all!" cried Bet. "You've not *just* missed her. That's why I must tell you about the cockatoo—"

"I don't want to hear about parrots."

"Please," said Bet. "You'll see. The cockatoo makes all the difference."

"I doubt that."

"Please."

"Oh, go on, then!" Mr. Franklin was too crushed by disappointment to care.

"Miss X was a little girl when she was given this beautiful white cockatoo on the very day that the queen got married. So she decided to call it after the queen."

Mr. Franklin made an effort to respond: "Elizabeth . . . Pretty Betty instead of Pretty Polly, I suppose. Or Bessy. Or Bess." Suddenly he thought he saw an unexpected vanity in all this. "Or Bet, perhaps?" He was teasing her, but there was an unkind edge to the teasing.

"None of those names," said Bet. "She called it Vicky."

"Vicky?" Mr. Franklin was bewildered. "Why Vicky? That's short for Victoria."

"Yes."

"Victoria," said Mr. Franklin. "Queen Victoria?"

"Go on," Bet said encouragingly.

"But Queen Victoria died, an old lady, over a hundred years ago."

"Yes."

"Do you mean the mole is a *hundred years old*?"

"Oh, older than that," said Bet. "The mole knew Miss X when the Darwin book came out, first ever, and he was there before that, when the white cockatoo called Vicky was still alive. So, the mole says, add another fifty years, give or take a few."

"That makes *a hundred and fifty years*," Mr. Franklin whispered.

"And before that," said Bet, "the mole had to tunnel all the way down from Scotland into England; add, say, another hundred years."

"From Scotland into England," Mr. Franklin repeated. By now he was in a daze. "Add another hundred . . .

That makes *two hundred and fifty years . . .*"

"And before that he had to spend nearly fifty years, he said, just hanging around in Scotland, waiting."

"Another fifty. . . . That makes *three hundred years.* . . ."

"Yes," said Bet. "He's a good three hundred years old. Just roughly, of course."

Mr. Franklin gripped the edge of the kitchen table in front of him and very slowly got to his feet. He leaned forward toward Bet, as if in menace.

He said, "*A talking mole three hundred years old . . .* I do not believe it."

"Well," Bet said reasonably, "you've believed the talking part of it. The mole says you'll just have to accept the rest."

"Accept! How can I accept something so outrageous without any verification, any explanation whatsoever?"

"Oh, but there is an explanation!" Bet said. "The mole said you wouldn't like it, and you'd say there wasn't any such thing, and of course, there isn't any such thing now, but there was then, three hundred years ago, and it really worked then, and—"

"WHAT ARE YOU TALKING ABOUT?"

In a very small voice, because she was frightened, Bet said: "Witchcraft."

Mr. Franklin said, "I thought you said witchcraft."

"I did," said Bet.

Mr. Franklin fell forward over the kitchen table in a dead faint.

"Granny!" Bet shouted, and Mrs. Allum came.

IX

THE LITTLE GENTLEMAN

"I WAS BORN," said the mole, "in or about the year 1700, at Hampton Court, outside London, in the reign of King William the Third. That is really the only thing in my early life of which I can be absolutely certain."

Bet sighed. This was, she knew, the one thing that Mr. Franklin would absolutely refuse to believe. A mole three hundred years old, and the only explanation offered: witchcraft!

Bet and the mole were talking, as usual, by the log. Most of the talk was by the mole; he was now frankly revealing to Bet all—or nearly all—that he knew of his own history. There was much that he had previously only hinted at, or told in part. Some of it, of course, Bet had already guessed.

Meanwhile, Mr. Franklin, with Moon as his only companion, had shut himself indoors; he had a large bruise on his forehead where his head had hit the kitchen table when he fainted. He was still deeply upset in his mind about what he had been told. As a result, he had no wish to talk with the mole again; he would not even pick up his binoculars to spy on him. Nowadays, if anyone checked on the meadow, it would have to be Mrs. Allum as she went about her housework.

"Witchcraft," said the mole, "of the most repulsive kind touched my life at only two points in time. The first was when my life span was extended—not for *my* benefit, note—into a future of no fixed duration."

"Everlasting life," breathed Bet.

The mole snarled at the phrase.

He went on. "On the second occasion, much later, I was by witchcraft given speech and the power of understanding, and with that power came memory. Of the time before that time, I have no real—no *steady*—memory. I partly rely on hearsay, the hearsay of a royal death and of a confusion of conspiracy and battle, and I—an innocent mole—caught in the midst of it all!

"I once asked Miss X to disentangle my very early history for me. Obligingly, she tried, but left me still perplexed. What she knew best, from the poems of

Tennyson, were the legends of Sir Lancelot and the other knights of King Arthur's Round Table, and their ladies. And they all belonged—if, indeed, they ever existed—to a time long, long before I was born."

"Couldn't Master Y help?" asked Bet.

"An agreeable boy," said the mole, "but interested only in the present, *his* present—and his future. He wanted to grow up and learn to fly, and so indeed he did. Not, you understand, like a bird, but in some kind of machine."

"And Mr. Franklin?" asked Bet. Then, hurriedly: "Sorry. Of course, he couldn't possibly have . . . "

"No," said the mole.

Timidly Bet asked, "What about me?"

"Do you know any early-eighteenth-century British history?"

"No, but perhaps I could find out something, from books at school."

"I should be grateful," the mole said simply. He added, "A clue. What Miss X told me left my mind in a fog of claimants and usurpers, daughters and cousins, plots and spies, and I don't know what else. But there seemed to be someone at the bottom of it all called Jacob, or possibly Jacobus."

"Jacob, or Jacobus," said Bet. "I'll remember."

The next Book Day, at school, Bet presented herself with the book that she wanted to borrow, Volume III of the *Encyclopedia of Homeland Histories*. She was feeling triumphant.

On the point of checking the book out to her, Miss Macduff paused and frowned. "This is a reference book, Bet. You forget. You're not allowed to borrow reference books, such as encyclopedias, to take home with you. Can't you read and make notes in school for whatever project you've been given?"

"It's not exactly a project," said Bet. "It's something

I wanted to read aloud to someone who's blind. He can't read for himself."

"Oh," said Miss Macduff. "Who is this person?"

In a panic, Bet said, "He's very old—"

"Your grandfather?"

"No, but he is a relative." She was remembering the mole's "freely and equally, *as mammal to mammal.*"

"And your grandmother knows all about your reading aloud to this elderly blind relative?"

"Oh, yes!" cried Bet, delighted to be sure of what she was saying.

"Still, you can't borrow a reference book," said Miss Macduff. She saw Bet's disappointment. "I tell you what: If you show me the page or pages—"

"Only one page," said Bet. "Here."

"I'll make a photocopy for you. It's the entry on Jacobites? Right." Suddenly Miss Macduff was smiling at Bet. "The Jacobites are part of the history of

Scotland, you know. Perhaps your old gentleman is Scottish?"

"No," said Bet. "He lived a long time in Scotland, but I think he didn't enjoy it there. He was born in England."

"Ah, well," said Miss Macduff.

The next day Bet sat by the log reading from the photocopy to an attentive mole:

"JACOBITES. So called from the Latin *Jacobus,* for the English name, *James.* The JACOBITES remained loyal to King James II when he was forced to abandon the throne and go into exile during the Revolution of 1688."

"Only a little before my time," said the mole, "and no doubt relevant. Continue, please."

So Bet read on:

" 'The JACOBITES plotted in England and in Scotland (where they were strongest) to get James II back on the throne, or—after his death—his only son, as King James III. Meantime, however, James II had been succeeded on the throne by a Dutch cousin, William, and his wife, Mary, who was daughter to James II.'"

"I told you it was complicated," said the mole.

"When Queen Mary died, her husband reigned alone, as King William III."

"Aha!" said the mole.

"The King was elderly and already ill when, in February 1702, he went riding in the park at Hampton Court—"

"This is it!" cried the mole, in the greatest excitement. "Go on, go on!"

" 'His horse stumbled on a molehill, and the king fell, hurting himself badly. A few weeks later he died. The JACOBITES were overjoyed at the news. Ever afterward they would drink secretly a health to "the little gentleman in black velvet," that is to say, to the mole whose molehill had led indirectly to the king's death.'"

"And is that all about the molehill and the mole?" asked the mole.

"Yes," said Bet. "But there's still quite a bit more about how the Jacobites still didn't get their way after the death of King William, because he was succeeded by Queen Anne. And after her it was King George I, a distant cousin from Germany, and then his son, another George, but the Jacobites went on hoping and hoping and plotting and plotting—"

The mole interrupted her: "But there's no more about the mole in Hampton Court Park? It seems to me there should be more. I am sure of it. . . ."

"No," said Bet. "There's no more."

"Nothing about a Jacobite spy in the royal household who was secretly to take the news of King William's death to Scotland, and resolved to take that mole, too, as living talisman and trophy?"

"No," said Bet.

"Nothing about how a mole in the park was trapped and caged and carried on horseback, posthaste, hundreds of miles north into Scotland?"

"No," said Bet. Then, horrified: "That mole was you? Oh, how cruel!"

"By the time we reached Scotland, I was as good as dead," said the mole. "But the Jacobites would not give up their idea of a living trophy, a mascot, as Master Y would have said. They must see what Scottish witchcraft could do for a dying mole." As he continued with his account, sketchy as it was, his voice began to shake. "They took me to high, open, lonely ground; a wind prowled there like a hungry beast. The nearness of death sharpened all my senses. There was a fire—I could feel the heat of it. On the fire stood some kind of cooking pot, for I could smell cooking—oh! but of a vile kind! Then old, old bony fingers seized me; my poor tail was cut off at its root and flung into that dreadful cooking pot—I heard the little plop! as it went in. Later they forced a drop of that same vile witch's brew down my throat. Thus they brought me back to life and made sure I would not—*could* not—die. They put me back into my cage to live on, no hope of death. . . . "

Bet's silence did not mislead the mole into thinking that she did not feel for him. He said, "When they remembered, they gave me food and water. Sometimes they cleaned out the cage."

Bet managed to ask, "How long was it?"

The mole asked, "How long did the book say that the Jacobites went on plotting and hoping to no purpose?"

"Just over forty years."

"Forty years, then," said the mole.

He could hear Bet catching her breath, trying not to

cry. "Don't grieve now, child. It's over, done with. Long, long ago. And I have yet to tell you of my second painful encounter with witchcraft and the outcome of that."

"No. Please," said Bet. "Not now. Not yet."

She could hardly speak for the anguish she felt. She had never before not wanted to hear him, to hang on his words.

"Very well," said the mole. "Later."

That—for the time being—was that.

X

THE BAG OF TRICKS

NEVER before had Bet doubted what the mole had told her, but this time she did not want to believe. Over forty years in a cage, fed and watered "when they remembered"! She could not bear to believe it.

In the time that followed and for a long time after

that, Bet used to look in books for anything to con-
tradict—or confirm—the mole's story. Sometimes—
but not often—she found something about the
Hampton Court molehill and the Jacobite toast to
"the little gentleman in black velvet." She never found
anything about a mole trapped and kept alive, a cap-
tive for over forty years, by witchcraft.

Yet she always knew in her heart that the mole's
story that day must be true. The mole would never lie
to her. So there was no escape for her; she must endure
in her imagination the knowledge of what had happened long ago.

That night, in her grandparents' house, Bet could not
sleep for such imaginings. The room was stuffy with
summer heat, so she got out of bed to open the window
to its widest and to draw the curtains right back.

In bed again, she hovered on the edges of sleep. If
she closed her eyes, immediately she began to see what

the mole had told her of: King William's horse stumbling on the molehill at Hampton Court, and the king's fall to his death; the headlong ride of the Jacobite spy from London into Scotland, with a dying mole caged up at his saddlebow; and, lastly, the midnight scene on the Scottish moor, with the bony-fingered witch and her bubbling cauldron.

On that moor, what the mole had only heard and smelled and felt by touch Bet *saw*. She was there; she saw it all. She saw the figures of people silhouetted black against the firelight. Among them was a man with a cage, and beside him a young boy, of about Bet's age. Between them they were forcing some little creature back into their cage, alive: the mole.

Then something quite different began to happen. The same man pushed his son forward to the witch and her cauldron. The child had a tiny leather pouch with a leather drawstring, just big enough to hold a single silver coin. The boy gave his coin to the witch, and in return she ladled into the pouch a thick black substance, now semisolid, from the cauldron. The boy drew the pouch string tight and went back to his father, who hung the little bag around the child's neck as a charm.

Even in her dream, Bet knew that what she had just seen was more than the mole had ever told her. In dream time she had been witness to a happening of three hundred years ago. But that midnight scene— moorland and witch and cauldron—now vanished in a senseless whirling rush of time that blew her back- ward—not centuries but millions of years—to the terri- fying sound of monster footsteps: *thump! thump! thump!*

Of course, a dinosaur! A dinosaur was coming to get her, and she could not run from it! She could not move!

Thump! thump! thump!

The thumping woke her from her nightmare. She was lying in bed in a sweat of fear, with the full moon shining on her face through the uncurtained, open window. Her grandmother had always said that moonlight brought bad dreams.

Thump—thump—thump.

Her grandfather was thumping on the floor beside his bed with his walking stick, which he kept to hand for just such a purpose. He slept alone in the double bed in the room across the landing. Directly below his bedroom was the front room of the Allum's house, never used unless for entertaining visitors. Here Mrs. Allum regularly slept on a makeshift bed, ever since her husband's complaints about her snoring. If he needed her, he thumped for her.

The trouble was that Mrs. Allum was deaf in one ear. If she happened to turn in her sleep, so that her good ear was buried in the pillow, she could not hear the knocking.

This must have happened now.

As well as thumping, old Mr. Allum was calling in what

voice he could wheezily manage: "Girl, girl, fetch her! Fetch her!"

Bet knew that she must run downstairs at once to wake her grandmother. Then, while Mrs. Allum was puffing her way upstairs, Bet put a kettle on to boil in the kitchen. For his asthmatic condition, Mr. Allum insisted on old-fashioned steam inhalations. By the time his wife had attended to his needs and he was feeling better, it would be almost morning. Often Mrs. Allum would simply reboil the kettle for a cup of tea and then start her housework ahead of the usual routine.

Bet herself was always sent promptly back to bed ("School tomorrow, girl!") after the trip to the front room and to the kitchen. This time she lay awake, still held by a fear she could not understand. There was no monster, after all, so what was this dread at her very heart?

Then she remembered: her mother, whom—so soon—she was to meet for the first time. She dreaded that meeting. When she had told the mole of her fear, he had comforted her and given her sound, calming advice. She now made a deliberate effort to follow that advice. After a while she fell asleep.

In the meadow after school, with Bet's consent, the mole resumed the distressing story of his long imprisonment in Scotland. *Homeland Histories* had already told of the Jacobites' continued plotting for the restoration of the so-called king James III. In 1745 his son landed in Scotland, where he was welcomed as Bonnie Prince Charlie, and there he raised an army to march into England to claim the throne for his father. They never reached London but turned back halfway. They fought their last battle in Scotland, on Culloden Moor, against the mainly English army, led by the Duke of Cumberland, a younger son of King George II. The Jacobites were utterly defeated. With that the entry in *Homeland Histories* had ended.

"Their defeat mattered nothing to me," said the mole, "but, in the violence and terror that followed, my cage was trampled over by horsemen and broken, and I escaped. I escaped! My one intention then was to take to the earth and tunnel my way far from the battlefield and from Scotland altogether. But I was very weak from lack of food. I had the strength only to crawl out of the ruins of my cage. I was surrounded by the dead and the dying, one of whom had been my jailer for many years. He wore around his neck a charm in a tiny leather pouch with a leather drawstring. Can you visualize such an object?"

"I can," said Bet.

"The soft leather of this little bag was the first thing I came across, and it was edible. I began to nibble and gnaw at the leather."

"Wasn't there anything inside the bag?"

"There was, and in my haste to satisfy hunger I gave up nibbling and gnawing and swallowed the whole thing in one go, bag and contents, all."

"What did it taste like?" Bet asked faintly.

"Appalling. But I hardly cared, and whatever witch-craft was in that bag of tricks gave instant, overwhelming strength to my will to escape. I dived into the earth and began at once to tunnel. I tunneled all that day and for many, many days afterward. For days, months, years. On and on, skirting towns and villages as I came to them, swimming streams and lochs and even great rivers. On and on, always making southward out of that accursed land."

"You're glad you're not Scottish," said Bet.

"Not Scottish?"

"You were born in England, so you're English."

The mole said fiercely: "I am neither Scottish nor English. I am mole, *Talpa europaea*. My native land is the earth, the soil through which I go. I care nothing for monarchs and their quarrels. Thrones, countries, nationalities, patriotisms mean nothing to me. Nothing."

Then, for the sake of his listener, the mole calmed himself. "You are still very young," he said. "You have not experienced what I came to know. At the Battle of Culloden, the English forces were commanded, as I have told you, by the Duke of Cumberland. After that battle, he was known as Butcher Cumberland. This was only partly because of slaughter on the battlefield. The dead and the dying among whom I made my escape were not on the battlefield at all. Men, women, children, old and young, were killed and their homes burned to the ground. The earth through which I tunneled in the first days after the battle stank with human blood."

Bet could see that at the recall of what he had witnessed, the mole's body was shaken with fear and with pity.

Presently he continued: "You will easily credit that it took me many, many years to tunnel my way out of Scotland and into England. I believe, nearly a hundred.

Then, one morning in early summer, somewhere in the north of England, I was tunneling away, perhaps rather nearer the surface than usual, when I was attracted by the sound of a human voice. It was speaking rhythmically, in a way that made me shiver with pleasure. Then the voice stopped. Then it resumed in a different, particular way of speaking, which one uses (I later knew) when one talks to oneself. The speaker was alone.

"Cautiously I surfaced, and the voice stopped. I realized that whoever it was had observed me. It would have been natural then for a mole to retreat underground at speed, but whatever had been in that bag of tricks still worked in me as strongly as on Culloden Moor. I dared to stay where I was.

"Very quietly the voice said: 'Good afternoon, sir.'

"I did not understand the words, but I understood the tone, gentle and friendly. I wanted to respond to the speaker, who I judged to be a young woman or a girl. I struggled to respond but had no words at all. I had never, in all my life as a mole, been able to understand or to use the words of human beings—or wanted to until now.

"As I struggled in vain to communicate *something*, I felt her fingers touch me. She did not try to take hold of me or even to stroke me. Only the tips of her fingers touched my shoulder, but her touch and my will to speak—the two together—gave me power. At first I could only repeat her words—exactly.

"At that exact repetition she laughed a little. 'You must not call me sir,' she said. 'I am my father's only daughter, so you had better address me as Miss—' and then she added an English surname too difficult for me to attempt. Was it Featherstonehaugh, or perhaps Woolstenholmes? Some such. She saw my difficulty and with the greatest delicacy suggested that at least for the time being I should call her Miss X. I have done so ever since."

The mole sighed, but contentedly. "That meeting changed my life, enriching it over the many years of our friendship. All that first summer we talked, and she read aloud to me, usually poetry, and sometimes she sang. This all happened in a corner of the vicarage lawn secluded from inquisitive eyes. I still remember the smell of the lilac, the sound of bees. When winter came, we could rarely meet, but Miss X had her piano moved into a room overlooking the garden. Whenever she could, she played and sang with the window open even in the coldest weather, so that I could hear her across the lawn. Winter or summer, year after year, we enjoyed each other's company, and I learned the art of human conversation."

There was a long pause; the mole seemed lost in recollection. But Bet, looking at him closely, saw that in the shade of his own doorway and in the safety of her presence, he had fallen happily asleep.

XI

THINGS HAPPEN

THE Saturday came for Bet and her grandmother to make their day trip to the East Anglian town of Disham to meet Bet's mother. This was the expedition that Bet had dreaded.

Old Mr. Allum disapproved of what they were

doing, but then, in the past, he had been too angry with his own daughter to allow her even to enter the house. Mrs. Allum, however, had become bold. She said that they were going, anyway, and that Mr. Allum could perfectly well manage without her for one Saturday: "With his dinner all laid ready for him, and his tea!"

Mrs. Allum was flustered by train travel and a strange town, but she had her daughter's address in her hand and, as she said, a tongue in her head. Eventually they reached the right block of council flats. They rang the bell at the front door, and Bet heard light, quick footsteps coming, and the door began to open—and opened. There stood her mother, at last.

Bet described the meeting later to the mole when she was back in the meadow. She and her mother had not at first embraced but only stared at each other as if they could hardly believe their eyes. Then, suddenly, awkwardly, they were hugging and kissing, and Mrs. Allum, to everyone's surprise, including her own, had wept.

"And then," Bet told the mole, "I met Jack, he's my mum's husband, he's a carpenter and joiner, and he works for a firm that does units and fitments in wood."

"Units and fitments in wood," repeated the mole, trying to grasp all that he was being told.

"And they have a baby. A little boy. He's my brother—well, my half brother. I've never had a brother before."

Bet had liked all that she had seen of her new family, and they had wanted Bet to come live with them. She wasn't quite sure.

"I cannot advise," said the mole. "As I once told you, moles have no experience of family life after their earliest infancy."

"My gran thought," said Bet, "that I might go and stay for a few days when the holidays begin. To see how we get on."

"A very reasonable step," said the mole.

"And then go again and stay longer."

"Well thought," said the mole.

"And then perhaps stay for good. They're getting a bedroom ready for me. It's going to be papered with roses on a trellis; and lovely shelves for books and things. Oh! and there's a girl called Madeleine—Maddy for short—who's my age, and she lives in the flat above, and her mum is friends with my mum."

"Excellent," said the mole. "Friends *and* family."

"But," said Bet emphatically, and paused.

"But?" said the mole.

"I'll come back often on visits to my gran, of course. And to see you."

"To see me . . . " the mole repeated thoughtfully.

"Yes," said Bet. She was too full of her news to pay attention to what the mole might be thinking. "And just supposing it doesn't work out with my mum, then my gran says I can come home to her and live just as before. If I really want to."

"Your grandmother is a woman of sound sense and a warm heart," said the mole.

"Yes," said Bet. "I suppose she is."

The long summer holidays were not so far away now. A date was fixed for Bet's second, longer visit.

As the time drew near, the mole became strangely disturbed at the prospect of Bet's absence. She tried to reassure him: "Only a week. Then I'm back."

The mole said, "I may not be here."

"Whyever not?"

In a moment the mole had become secretive; also short-tempered and sullen; hard. He said, "Things happen."

"But— what things?"

"Things." Then suddenly: "You seem not to realize that I have more important things to do than to loll here all day, chatting. I travel to a destination. I have to get to Hampton Court. I can't forever put that off. I must make a start on this last lap. Years of hard tunneling, no doubt, but still, the last lap."

Bet felt desperate. "But you wouldn't set off before I got back from my mum's? You wouldn't do that, would you?"

The mole would promise nothing. He was in a strange, contrary mood, very gloomy.

In despair Bet went to Mr. Franklin. Only after much hesitation had she resolved to consult him. Since the mention of witchcraft, they had never spoken together of the mole. Indeed, they had hardly spoken together at all. It was as if they were back in the time before Mr. Franklin's broken leg and his testing her ability to read aloud about earthworms.

Bet found Mr. Franklin sitting among his aunt's books, reading and making notes, with Moon for company. He tipped Moon off his usual chair, so that Bet could sit down. He saw that she had something important on her mind. He listened, and Bet found that he had not forgotten about the mole. On the contrary, Mr. Franklin had even come to accept the fact of the mole's great age.

"And you say he's thinking of going to Hampton Court?"

"Yes."

"Why?"

Bet was taken aback. She said that perhaps—well, after all, the mole had been born there.

Mr. Franklin snorted. "What a reason!"

With satisfaction Mr. Franklin went on to point out the impracticality of the idea: "To reach Hampton Court, he's got to get to the other side of London, does he realize that? He certainly can't take a direct route, straight across London, or he may well find himself trying to cast up a molehill under a stone lion in Trafalgar Square. No, he'll have to go right around London, and that will mean years and years of extra tunneling. Years and years and years. And then, when he gets to Hampton Court, does he realize that in the twenty-first century the whole place will be swarming with tourists? Oh! and I believe there's a golf course there nowadays, too. The golfers won't like molehills one little bit!"

Bet was dismayed. "What do you think, then? I mean, what should I say to him?"

"Ask him what I've asked you: Why?"

"Oh, dear!" said Bet. "I don't think he'll like my asking that."

XII

A USEFUL CURIOSITY

WHEN Bet got back to the mole, she found him, to her relief, in a very changed mood. She had hardly settled in the grass, leaning against the log, than he began to apologize for his previous surliness. "I dread absences," he explained.

"But I'll come back," protested Bet.

"So Master Y said." The mole sighed. "He was a young man by then. He went off to fly in his machine—to fight battles in the air, you know. He never came back. I think he died in the air, like a shot bird."

Steadily Bet repeated: "I'll come back."

"And Miss X—" said the mole, and stopped.

"Miss X?"

"In her absence I deserted her—so it must have seemed to her."

"What happened?"

"We had been friends for so many years," said the mole. "Miss X was growing into a middle-aged woman, still housekeeping for her old father, the vicar. She seldom left home. Occasionally a married brother in London would invite her on a long visit. Very occasionally she went.

"On the last occasion—"

The mole stopped speaking; he could not continue.

"Please, please, go on," begged Bet.

"On the last occasion," he said, "—oh, I shall never forget our parting on that last morning. Neither of us guessed what lay ahead. I bade her *au revoir* and urged her to enjoy the busy social life of London. I made some silly joke about my not knowing her when we met again, after her remarkable London experiences.

"And we never met again . . . "

The mole raised his whole head and shoulders in what Bet saw was an attitude of lamentation. And to her amazement she saw two teardrops form and force their way through the dense fur of his cheeks and roll downward. She knew from Mr. Franklin that moles were sightless but not eyeless. Eyes were present, but not quite fully formed—only rudimentary. That was Mr. Franklin's word: rudimentary.

Yet from these sightless eyes were forced the tears of true grief. She watched the impossible tears roll down the fur and fall.

"Never to meet again . . . " repeated the mole.

"But why, how?"

"Apparently over months, perhaps over several years, one of the undergardeners—a sharp lad—had heard us talking together, had spied on us. While Miss X was away, he took his chance—I all unaware of danger. He set his trap, caught me, and bundled me up to sell on as a useful curiosity to a traveling showman of his acquaintance. And so I was whisked far, far away from the vicarage and from any inquiries that might ever be made about my disappearance.

"I pleaded with the showman to release me—fool that I was! Of course, he was delighted to hear me speak so fluently and intelligently. He promised me all kind of rewards if I would perform in public—and threatened me with all kinds of torture if I would not. The only reward I wanted was my liberty. This, in the end, he promised, but by now I knew better than to trust him. He spoke of having 'a comfortable little waistcoat' made for me, but then I overheard him discussing it with a blacksmith. It was to be made of fine interlocking steel links—'better than any dog collar,' they said, for once on my body, it could never be taken off. To this would be attached a fine chain, again of steel. So I would never, never be able to escape.

"My only hope was to escape before the waistcoat was finished. I pretended to be eager to serve the showman at once, to begin earning my liberty, and he was greedy for immediate money. I was to perform for the first time at one of the regular fairs he visited on the outskirts of a busy manufacturing town.

"I remember that day very well. The showman had pitched our tent among all the other tents and booths and show carts. From inside the tent I could hear all the sounds of the fair, and particularly the sound of the townspeople gathering in greater and greater numbers for the fun. Some of them were rough customers. The showman was ringing his bell and shouting for people to come in to hear the Magic Mole, as he called me. He was busy collecting entrance money, and when he could get no more people inside the tent, all standing, he closed the flaps and told the audience that the performance would begin.

"I was already there in my iron cage—oh, yes! a cage—with a cloth thrown over it. The cage stood on a small wooden table at the far end of the tent from the spectators. They were kept from coming too close by some kind of makeshift barrier. They were a rowdy lot. I could hear them pressing against the barrier, swearing at it, and I thought with satisfaction, That can give! I could hear them, and I could also *smell* them. There was one loud-mouthed man at the very front—a huge man, I thought—a butcher, perhaps, for he smelled of blood as well as beer and sweat. He was drunk; that pleased me, too.

"There was another, faint smell that came from the

far side of the table away from the spectators. It rose from the ground in the narrow space between the table and the tent wall: the smell of crushed grass and the sweet smell of damp soil. That smell meant that there was no wooden flooring between me and the earth. That was of the greatest consequence.

"Meanwhile, the showman had opened the door of the cage and I had crept out. As we had agreed, I turned to face the audience and at the same time sat back on my hindquarters, like a dog begging." The mole shuddered.

"The showman asked me with much mock politeness to start the entertainment by singing 'God Save the Queen.'

"I did not respond. I did not utter a word. I did not part my lips or move a muscle of my body.

"The showman said quickly, mock-apologetic: 'O dearie dearie me! The little gentleman's shy!'

"The crowd roared with stupid laughter, but I also

heard the butcher shout, 'Get on with it; we want our money's worth!'

"The showman was rattled. I could smell the sweat on him, the fright. He didn't know what I was up to. He began to ask the questions we had rehearsed together —question and answer. But now I gave no answers to his questions. In desperation he pretended that I was speaking in a voice too tiny to be heard by anyone but him. But the people at the front of the crowd could see that my mouth remained tight shut, and the bully butcher began shouting, 'It's a fraud, a swindle!'

"The showman started to poke me and pinch me to make me speak, and the crowd, led by the butcher, began to roar in outrage. They cared nothing for the poor mole, but they wanted their revenge on this cheating showman. They shouted and jostled against the flimsy barrier until it creaked and jolted, and suddenly—crack!—it was down, and the drunken butcher and the whole lot of them were lunging forward on to the showman at his table.

"The showman was in fear for his life; I never knew what happened to him. Me—I had instantly flipped over the edge of the table farthest from the oncoming crowd, over and down to the lovely earth, and then I was tunneling like fury almost vertically down . . . down . . . while above me I heard the crashing and smashing of the table and the cries of the angry, struggling mob.

"And I left it all behind me, as I took myself deep into the earth—

"Deep—

"Safe—

"Free . . . "

After that last word, the mole let out a long sighing breath of relief, and Bet, carried by imagination into his story, seemed actually to smell the lovely earth around him and above him, always his protection and his freedom.

XIII

HOLY MOLE

THERE was a long silence by the log after the end of
the mole's story of hairsbreadth escape. Bet thought
that he was perhaps tasting again the success of the
trick he had used against the showman. Then he began
slowly to swing his heavy head from side to side, as if

to cast from it all such self-congratulation. Gloom now enwrapped him.

Bet said: "But you didn't mean to desert Miss X. You would have gone back to her if you could, but you didn't know the way. None of it was your fault."

"True," said the mole. He seemed no happier for the thought.

Now was the moment, Bet knew, for Mr. Franklin's question. She began: "And then you decided you must go to Hampton Court."

"I didn't suddenly decide that. I'd always known I must go. Even in Scotland, I'd known."

"But why?"

The mole did not answer.

"Was it because you had been born there?"

The mole gave a snort like Mr. Franklin's, but mole-sized. "Moonshine!" he said.

"Then why?"

She had to be answered. "Well," said the mole, "Hampton Court was the one place in the whole wide world that I knew how to get to."

"What do you mean?"

"Homing instinct. So Master Y once explained to me. Birds have it, particularly homing pigeons. In this respect, apparently, I resemble a homing pigeon." He paused, seeming not much to care for the comparison, then continued: "So I knew, without thinking, that I must tunnel my way out of Scotland into England, making always roughly south toward London and Hampton Court. Sometimes there were diversions, of course; also delays—those several delightful decades with Miss X, just over the Border, and then, farther south, a good few years with Master Y in what he told me was the Vale of York (such fertile soil—most excellent earthworms!); and now here, further south still, with you. Even a homing pigeon would have to grant that I am still making in the right direction."

The mole was pleased with himself. He thought he had dealt with Bet's awkward question Why?

Bet, however, had been thinking carefully. She said: "If you know the way to a place, that doesn't mean that you have to go there."

"No," admitted the mole.

"So that's a silly reason, too."

"Well, yes," said the mole.

"So—*why?*"

The mole, saying nothing, drew himself together and began to inch his body backward into his tunnel.

In a panic, Bet cried, "Don't go! Please, don't go! I'm sorry I bothered you with questions. Oh, please, stay!"

He stayed. He said gruffly, "A friend has a right to ask questions. But to answer may be too complicated, too hard."

Silence followed this speech; Bet listened carefully

to it. Finally she said, "It's because of the witchcraft, isn't it?"

The mole's body shook with the force of his reply. "Yes! By now—oh! what I want most in this world is to get that accursed witchcraft out of my blood and my bones and my brain and my fur and my feet—oh, to be rid of it utterly! To be as I was before that single drop of witch's brew first touched my tongue in Scotland, and before, all unknowing, I swallowed that whole abominable little bag of tricks on Culloden Moor! To be myself again, pure mole, as I was at Hampton Court before the king's horse stumbled at the molehill. My only hope is to get back to Hampton Court *to meet myself there*, to be myself again, as I was then!"

Bet said quietly and sadly, "Three hundred years ago . . . "

But the mole paid no attention—if he heard. He ranted on. "As I was then, pure mole—all of me mole—nothing taken from me by witchcraft, nothing added by witchcraft—"

Something echoed in Bet's mind from stories of courtroom trials and witnesses sworn to tell "the truth, the whole truth, and nothing but the truth."

Aloud she said: "Mole, wholly mole, and nothing but mole."

The mole was startled. "Holy mole? Myself with halo?"

Bet was surprised, too. "You've made a pun."

"A pun?"

"A kind of joke." She ventured to laugh.

He was not interested, but he was not offended either, and for a moment he had been diverted from the passionate outpouring of his rage and regret and his clutched-at hopes. He was calmer. He could listen to reason.

Bet said: "That first single drop from the witch's

cauldron brought you back to life, gave you the power to live, perhaps forever, perhaps in captivity forever. That was bad, and that was sad."

"Alas!" said the mole. "Alas, alas!"

"But the bag of tricks gave you powers of different kinds that you could really use."

"Did it?" He still desponded but was glad to have the tangle of his past experiences sorted out for him.

"Didn't you escape on Culloden Moor and from the showman's tent by tunneling deeper and faster—and *sheer* down—than you could ever have done if you had been an ordinary mole? You said so yourself, I think.'"

"Did I?" said the mole, a little cheered. "Yes, I think that's true."

"And then," said Bet, "the bag of tricks gave you the power of language, the power to talk—no, before that it gave you the power to *want* to talk, to imagine being able to talk. So that when you met Miss X, you were ready to try talking to her, and you did talk to her. So you made friends with Miss X, and then, later, with Master Y."

"And now with you," said the mole. "For which I am grateful. And yet—" He was afraid of appearing ungrateful after all, or rude. He said: "A capacity for human friendship is not part of being a mole—true, pure mole."

"But it is not a bad thing," said Bet.

"Perhaps not," said the mole. "But it is not a mole thing."

Bet did not argue. She said: "That's what witchcraft added. Did it take anything away?"

"Have you forgotten?" He had crept out of his hole again, so that now his entire body was visible to Bet. "You see me?"

"Yes," said Bet, puzzled.

"But you have forgotten. You think you see the

whole of me from the tip of my nose to—to—"

"Oh!" cried Bet. "Your poor tail! It's not there! It was cut off and thrown into the witch's cauldron. Oh, I'm so sorry!"

The mole said, "A mole's life is in the digging of tunnels and in the going to and fro along the tunnels he has made, and he makes those tunnels exactly to fit the size and shape of his body. The brushing of my body against the sides and the roof of a tunnel gave to my whole being a delicious sensation that was more than mere pleasure, more even than happiness. That was when I had a tail. The tail was short and thin and held aloft to touch sides and roofs of tunnels and so complete the circuit of content within my body. I lost that completion when I lost my tail. Without it I can never be wholly mole."

Bet said slowly, "Yes, I see. I *think* I see." She had glimpsed, as far as she—a human being—was able to, what it felt like to be another kind of being altogether: a mole. She saw, even if only a little way, into mole nature, and that insight allowed her to feel for this mole—to feel *with* him his anxiety, his longing to be wholly and only and utterly himself: mole.

Her shadowy and confused thinking was broken into by the mole. With glum briskness he was saying, "Well, I suppose that what cannot be cured must be endured. According to Miss X."

"Oh, no!" cried Bet. "There must be a way. Give me time. I can think of something. In fact, already—"

There she broke off and for the time being would say no more.

XIV

THE EXPERIMENT

"LISTEN CAREFULLY," Bet said, resuming the conversation with the mole exactly where she had left it.

"I'm listening."

"You have witchcraft in you. You want to get rid of it—to get rid of every little bit of it, don't you?"

"Yes," said the mole.

"But you can see no way of getting rid of it."

"True, alas!" said the mole.

"But the witchcraft itself is power. It's in you, so it belongs to you. It's yours. You can use it."

"Can I?"

"Of course you can. It's only a matter of finding out how exactly to use it. You must experiment—try out. And then practice. In the end, you'll get so good at using it that at last"—Bet paused for emphasis—"you can use the witchcraft in you to get rid of the witchcraft in you. Just like that."

"Use the witchcraft to get rid of the witchcraft . . . " repeated the mole. "But experiment? How would I experiment—try out, as you say?"

"Easy," said Bet. "For instance, you could begin with me. You once said that if I'd been small enough, you'd have shown me your tunnels underground."

The mole did not see the direction the conversation was taking. He said gravely, "Had you been of a suitable size, I would have been honored to escort you underground."

"Then try shrinking me—now!"

Startled, the mole wailed, "Don't rush me!" But that was exactly what Bet wanted to do. Otherwise, she thought, if he were given time, the mole would think up a dozen excuses never to meddle with the witchcraft in him.

She repeated, coaxing this time: "*Please*, shrink me." As she spoke, with the tip of one finger she touched the mole, as Miss X had touched him long ago into friendship.

The mole wavered but could not resist such an appeal. With Bet's finger still resting lightly on him, he said, "For you, I'll try. I'll try—now!" His whole body stiffened with the gathering of his will to match Bet's will.

She gave a little gasp, a whisper: "I think—oh, I think something's beginning to happen!"

And at that very moment from across the pasture came Mrs. Allum's voice: "Bet, can you hear me? It's time to be off. Bet! Bet!"

Bet was saying to the mole, "It worked, it worked! I feel smaller; you'd begun to shrink me! Oh, it worked!" She had jumped to her feet with excitement—and also in response to her grandmother's calling. She must go.

"You can't go!" cried the mole. "I must undo what I've done. You can't go home *shrunk*."

"No time!" said Bet. "And shrunk such a tiny bit, no one will notice. We'll sort things right when we next meet."

And she was dancing away across the meadow in the highest spirits, to where Mrs. Allum was waiting for her.

Mrs. Allum stared at her granddaughter. "You look

peaky," she said. "I don't know what your mum will think when she next sees you. I hope you've caught nothing off that dratted mole. Do you feel poorly?"

"No," said Bet. "I'm all right. I feel specially all right."

Mrs. Allum appealed to Mr. Franklin, who had just come from his study with a book in his hand. Mr. Franklin, peering uncertainly, thought that Bet looked much as usual.

Mrs. Allum was dissatisfied. She said nothing more in the car on the way home, but as soon as she saw her husband, she began again. "Look at the girl! What's wrong with her?"

Old Mr. Allum was impatient for his tea. He glanced at Bet. "There's nothing wrong with her—oh, well, yes, she's shrunk a little."

"She's *what?*"

He shouted, "Woman, she's *shrunk*, and I want my tea!"

"Shrunk?" Mrs. Allum was dumbfounded. "Of course, she hasn't shrunk! Children don't shrink, they grow. Shrunk, indeed! She just needs feeding up." And Mrs. Allum gave Bet two poached eggs on toast to go with her tea.

Bet's size had to be delicately readjusted at the very next meeting between herself and the mole. But they were both aghast at the risk they had taken so unthinkingly.

For, on impulse, they had experimented with shrinkage in broad daylight in full view of the cottage. They were lucky that Mrs. Allum had not noticed what they were up to.

In the future, they must do any experimenting and practice out of sight *behind* the log, instead of in front of it. That seemed a straightforward solution to their problem, but best perhaps not to make this move too obvious, too noticeable.

Already Mrs. Allum's suspicions had been roused. She had a feeling that some kind of mischief was going on in the meadow. And if Bet looked smaller— *thinner*—was her health at risk in some way? What might her mother have to say? Mrs. Allum decided that Bet must regularly take a mug of milk with her to drink on the log. From the cottage Mrs. Allum could watch her drink it.

To begin with, Bet sat on the log, facing the river and drinking her milk.

On her next visit she took her milk and sat on the ground behind the log, with the log at her back. From the cottage her grandmother could see the top of a head, and pretty soon a hand came up to leave an empty mug in place on the log.

So that was still all right, more or less, from Mrs. Allum's point of view.

But, on yet another visit, Bet lay down on the

ground. She had often done this before in front of the log, but now she was behind it, quite out of sight. Mrs. Allum stared and waited. In due course a hand appeared and left the mug on the log. And that was that.

"I don't like it," said Mrs. Allum.

The next time Bet disappeared from view in this way, Mrs. Allum resolved to visit the log. She did not call Bet's name as she started out.

The mole had just managed to reduce Bet to about nine-tenths of her normal size when from across the meadow, they heard the grind and creak of the gate being opened. They acted at once. They were becoming quite skilled at shrinkage and reexpansion, and the process was no longer jerky and unpredictable. By the time Mrs. Allum loomed over the log, Bet had been returned to her usual appearance and was seemingly asleep on the grass, while the mole was out of sight in his tunnel.

Without a word Mrs. Allum picked up the empty mug and went back to the cottage. A day or two later she tried again—without success.

By now the mole's nerves were on edge. He refused to practice shrinkage for more than a short time and then only to an easily reversible degree. When would they ever have enough time—calm time—for what they planned?

Then chance favored their hopes. Mr. Franklin was going to London for the day to consult some rare book in the British Library.

Bet suggested to Mr. Franklin that this was just the right moment, while he was in London, to let her grandmother clean his study. Mrs. Allum had not been allowed to touch the room since he had first moved into the cottage. Mr. Franklin himself admitted that by now it was a mess.

Before he left for his day in London, he could stack

his books and pile his papers, and then, as Bet pointed out to him, Mrs. Allum would have several uninterrupted hours to sweep and mop and dust and polish.

"But, please, don't tell my gran that it was my idea."

"Why not?"

"*Please.*"

"Very well."

There was still the possibility that Mrs. Allum would break off, even from this most urgent cleaning, to see what might be going on at the log. Suppose she found nobody there?

"But I think I can gain us time against such an eventuality," said the mole. His idea was to dig a new side tunnel from his main system, to come up behind one of the five big trees in the meadow, in a spot partly concealed by a branch recently fallen, still in full leaf. "By the time your grandmother has seen that you're not behind the log, you'll be your proper size behind the ash tree. She'll be in a muddle in her mind, but at least she'll have found you, safe and well."

"Will she notice anything? Shall I be very dirty from having been underground?"

"Not *dirty*." He was hurt at the suggestion. "Somewhat earthy, perhaps."

Bet had one last worry. "Just suppose it pours with rain, so that my gran won't let me go into the meadow at all?"

"Ah," said the mole.

This was a heat wave, however, that would not break for some time yet.

CHTHONIC

T HE mole was proud of what he called his word. He had had it from Miss X. It must be pronounced like *sonic*, but with a lisp at the beginning: *chthonic*. Miss X had even taught him the surprising spelling: c-h-t-h-o-n-i-c.

"And there really is such a word?" said Bet.

"Indeed, there is. Miss X used it of *me* and of my residence underground."

The mole and Bet were resting by the log after some practice at the early stages of shrinkage, and the mole was trying to prepare Bet for her descent into his tunnel system.

He said: "*Chthonic* is the word used to describe an underworld beneath the surface of the earth. Such a world was well known to the Greek gods in ancient times. So Miss X told me, and she learned of it from her father, the vicar, who was a Greek scholar. The word comes from the Greek."

"But there are no Greek gods there now?"

"No," said the mole, "but who knows whom—or what—you may otherwise *chthonically* meet? Whatever happens, I shall be with you; you will have nothing to fear. And remember, you are probably the first human being ever to be so privileged."

Bet still worried. "Shall I have to meet your friends?"

"My *friends?*"

"You once said that in a pasture this size there would be other moles with their own tunnels. Shall I have to meet some of them?"

The mole said: "Moles have no friends. Each mole has his—or her—own tunnel system. If one mole wanders into another mole's tunnel, there is a fight—if necessary, to the death. The only exception to this is in early spring, when a male seeks out a female to mate with. So the mole race can continue." The mole sighed heavily. "But this also witchcraft has deprived me of— the wish and the ability to procreate. However,"—his tone brightened—"I have my tunnels still. Alone I dig them; alone I live in them."

"It sounds rather sad," said Bet.

"No," said the mole. "This is mole nature. Human nature is different. Human beings seem to need friends. You must always have had friends."

Bet thought, Not really, but said nothing. Old Mr. Allum did not like the idea of strangers, as he would have called them, coming to the house, and Mrs. Allum did not like Bet to go visiting alone. But everything would be different when she was with her family in Disham. For one thing, Maddy would be a friend; Bet was almost sure of that.

By now, the thought of her next visit—a stay of several days and nights with her family—did not worry Bet at all. She looked forward to it. And before that there would be this extraordinary—this *amazing*—experience of venturing down into the mole's subterranean and labyrinth-like private residence, his chthonic home.

The day of the great underground adventure dawned fine, with a promise of heat later. Mr. Franklin went to London. Mrs. Allum devoted herself to the spring-cleaning—out of season—of Mr. Franklin's study.

And the mole and Bet began to carry out their plan.

They had practiced shrinkage and reexpansion many times, but only to very limited size changes. "Now," said Bet with satisfaction, "we're going to go the whole hog."

"More accurately," said the mole, "the whole mole!" He laughed at his own joke, but nervously. He had admitted to Bet his fear that in reducing her to mole size, he might (as he put it) "overdo things" and obliterate her entirely. But Bet trusted him.

The beginning of shrinkage had become easy and smooth. This time, however, the pressure of the mole's will and of Bet's will, linked through finger touch, had to continue far beyond that. They willed on together, and steadily Bet saw the log beside her grow upward into a brown, rugged escarpment, at the foot of which she cowered, awed. The grasses became head-high green lances; a buttercup towered above her.

She had an overwhelming, dizzy, headachy feeling,

and above all, she felt afraid—afraid of everything so unexpectedly big and threatening, and her own self so small and so defenseless.

The mole's voice, on a level with her ear, was comforting. "The sooner we are down below, the better it will be for you. Follow me."

He made for his tunnel mouth, and Bet forced herself to follow him, scurrying through the grasses like the unlikely, terrified little creature she was.

"Follow!" and the mole was disappearing down his hole. Bet took a breath and followed, dropping on hands and knees as she did so.

For a very short time daylight still reached them; then all was darkness.

The mole had been right. Once belowground and in the dark, the headachy feeling and the fear left her. Always just ahead of her she heard the mole's voice: "Follow."

She was aware that she had become molelike in more than size only. She had entered the mole's passageway on hands and knees, but that seemed to change. It was easier and faster to go on all fours, like any other four-footed animal, large or small. And the darkness: she was not sure whether the darkness around her was something she saw or something that was there because her eyes were shut. She was not sure about her eyes. She tried to touch an eye but could not find it. Without alarm, she wondered whether her eyes were now *furred over*. She was not certain whether she was girl or partly mole—most likely, perhaps, both at once. She found that she did not mind in the least.

"Follow," said the mole.

The air in the tunnel was pleasantly cool after the heat of the blazing sun outside, and the walls and roof of the tunnel were cool as she brushed against them. She could feel the earth firm-packed but not hard, and its outer surface often had a satiny feel as of a very thin skin that could be broken through almost at a touch. A brief sound ahead, more of a slithering than a scrabble, suggested that something was indeed coming through—some tiny living creature—and she felt the mole pause and heard his jaws snap, and then he mumbled, "Delicious!" before moving on.

"Follow," he said again, and they branched off into a side shaft, and the floor beneath Bet began gently to slope downward. Her foot knocked against something embedded in the floor. For a moment she thought it must be some kind of paving stone. But no, it felt metallic, and the edge that poked from the earth was curved. She called the mole back to ask him about it. "You would be surprised," he said, "at what is let fall in a pasture, and whatever it is then works down into the earth. Perhaps, say, a button."

What an enormous button! Bet thought doubtfully,

and then she remembered her own size.

"Follow," called the mole, from ahead, and Bet hurried to catch up with him again. The floor of the tunnel still sloped down—down.

She followed, but she was often lingering like a traveler in a strange land, wanting to miss nothing: the layers of curious smells, none of them offensive to a girl who was also part mole; the heavy silence and then the minute sounds of movement; the feel of earth above, below, around. They were now certainly much deeper underground than they had been before.

She had dawdled, and suddenly she was no longer aware of the mole ahead. That friendliness had gone. She seemed to have entered—or had it come up around her?—a kind of hollow, booming blacker-than-blackness that now filled the tunnel from side to side, from floor to top. It was like a huge wave, a high tide, an ocean that flowed around her and through her.

It had no voice, and yet she heard its singing:

Mole—
Tunnel digger—
Hill raiser—
Worm hunter—
Brother battler—
Earth master—
Mole—

She crouched on the floor of the tunnel overwhelmed, speechless, until at last whatever it was had ebbed or thinned or seeped away and finally had gone. Then the mole was there again. "Something wrong?"

"What—oh, what was it?" whispered Bet.

"What was what?"

She could not possibly describe it properly. "A huge sort of . . . partly a booming—no, an echo of something like—oh! a *noise* that I never . . . ever—"

"The tunnels are full of noises, and moles are an ancient race, older far than any Greek gods. Take heart. Follow, and I'll show you a curiosity."

Still fearful, she followed him closely now. They crept for some way along a main tunnel and then along shafts branching off and upward again. "Here's one of my worm larders." "This is my sleeping chamber. The dry grass and leaves I bring from aboveground." At last they came to a place where their tunnel seemed to open up into a solemn emptiness.

"Find the walls," whispered the mole. "Feel them."

Bet groped to one side. "Pillars," she said, also in a whisper. "Curved pillars."

"Of bone," said the mole. "And a bone roof ridge above you. We are inside the rib cage of a dog buried here many years ago. Only bones remain. Franklin's aunt had a dog, long before Moon was even a kitten. He was handsome, sweet-tempered and golden-coated, so she called him Sunny. He died, and she buried him here. He was much loved, I think."

"How do you know all that?"

"The bones sing in the earth. Listen. Can't you hear them?"

Bet listened; then "No," she said sadly.

"Never mind." They stood side by side in silence, respectfully, as if they were in a cathedral. Everything was so still that even Bet felt the tremor in the earth that made the mole say in a low voice, "People are walking above us! We are not far from the field gate. Franklin must be back early from London and—yes, two sets of footsteps . . . the others could be your grandmother. We must get back at once—to the tree exit, I think. Hurry, hurry!'

Bet hurried back along the way they had come, with the mole giving directions from behind her as he followed closely. "Right turn ahead. Now we're in the main tunnel again. Left ahead! Now right and sharply up! You should be seeing daylight at any minute—"

"I can!" gasped Bet.

"As soon as you're outside, we'll start the expansion."

But "Now, now!" screamed Bet in the tiny voice of part mole, part shrunken child. For outside she could just perceive, waiting, the face, astonished yet fiercely intent and eager, of Moon.

XVI

THE RIGHT SIZE

FROM Bet's cry of "Now!" the mole understood that—for some appalling reason—there was no time to wait until she was fully outside for their reversal of shrinkage. The two things had to be simultaneous.

In panic the mole brought all his will to power with

violent suddenness and held it there. The result was extraordinary. Even as Bet scrabbled toward daylight, she was swelling, swelling, and the compression of the tunnel walls around her forced her forward fast and then still faster. In a shower of earth and also twigs and leaves she burst out of the mole hole like a cork out of a champagne bottle.

With a screech Moon had fled; for him this was a hundred times worse than the attack with *The Complete Poetic Works of Alfred Lord Tennyson in One Volume*. Startled by the caterwaul, the two people at the log looked around.

"There she is!" cried Mr. Franklin, and Mrs. Allum exclaimed, "Why's she *there* and not here?" And then: "Something's wrong!" Together they set off in alarm to Bet's prostrate form. She was lying with eyes closed and her face an almost greenish white, and damp. Her breathing was irregular and gasping.

Mr. Franklin questioned poor, distracted Mrs. Allum

about epilepsy or any other kind of fit. "Never!" said Mrs. Allum. "God forbid!"

Meanwhile, Bet was recovering with perhaps surprising speed. Her eyes opened and looked around. The color came back to her face, and her breathing steadied. There were two odd things about her, which Mr. Franklin noticed, but Mrs. Allum gave them little importance.

Bet was staring about her, in doubt. She asked faintly, "Which am I?"

"You mean," Mr. Franklin said gently, "'Where am I?' You're in the meadow, under the ash tree."

"Don't bother the girl with talk!" said Mrs. Allum. "Oh! I must get her to a doctor or hospital!"

"No!" cried Bet with sudden vigor. She scrambled to her feet to show how well she was and stood, swaying slightly.

Mr. Franklin now made his second observation: "She really does seem to have grown since this morning."

The sight of Bet on her feet again calmed Mrs. Allum at once. She could even respond to Mr. Franklin's last remark. She said, "It's only what I tell *him*. Children grow."

Bet seemed well enough to be asked the obvious question: "What happened?" But her answer was so confused that Mr. Franklin and Mrs. Allum together decided this was perhaps just a case of too much sun.

Bet was escorted carefully back to the cottage, where she was made to lie down for a while in a darkened room with her feet propped higher than her head. She was glad to lie there alone, while her whole body finished settling down into itself. Her bones, in particular, still felt shaken and sore.

She could hear her grandmother and Mr. Franklin talking elsewhere in the cottage, in lowered voices—probably about her.

She longed to be allowed back into the meadow by

herself. She needed to reassure the mole that in spite of such a frantic expansion, she was all right. She also wanted to point out—perhaps he realized this already—that he had proved his power over the witchcraft in him. Even, indeed, to excess. Now he knew for certain that he could use witchcraft to get rid of witchcraft, to become true mole again.

This last thought was hard for Bet. She had not allowed herself before now to admit what it meant. The mole had often told her that a true mole never sought human company, feared human beings, and would shun them. So their friendship would be over.

In the midst of her brooding, Mrs. Allum came to take her home. Bet had a bowl of bread and milk for her supper and then was put to bed, early as it was.

She was glad to be in bed, but she could not possibly sleep. Her size bothered her. Her feet reached to the very end of the bed, which they had never done before, and, if she wriggled her body up the bed, then at once her head hit the headboard. She was taller and altogether bigger than she should be; she felt *wrong*.

Her grandfather had stared at her almost disbelievingly and grunted. What would it be like at school when people saw her? What would Maddy think? Oh! What would her mum say?

There was nothing else for it. She must go back to the mole to ask to be restored to her normal size, and as soon as possible.

She dozed the evening away, resting. As soon as both her grandparents had gone to bed and she judged them to be safely asleep (her grandmother was snoring), she set off, leaving the front door on the latch for her return.

The night was light with starshine, and at any other time she would have enjoyed this solitary, secret expedition. But now she was too anxious and too ill at ease in her new size. She trudged wearily along the few miles that separated home from the Franklin cottage: first, along the high road, then a lane, and then the farm track. She knew that Mr. Franklin often worked very late, but the cottage was in darkness. She went into the meadow, to the log. There she sat down and then lay down on the dewy grass by the mole hole.

She called down the hole, but only softly, for fear of being heard in the cottage. There was no response. In her mind's eye she saw the mole curled up among the grass and leaves of the sleeping chamber that he had shown her, fast asleep. He would never hear her.

Then suddenly he was there, hauling himself very slowly up to the mouth of the tunnel, where he rested. He seemed glad that she had come, but he was still exhausted from his frenzied exertion face to face with Moon. He said, "I recognized your footsteps overhead. Heavier than usual. That's because you're bigger—too big. I'm sorry I bungled that. . . ."

"You saved me," said Bet. "From Moon. And without my help at all."

He shuddered. "At a cost. All—all my life's energy was spent in that moment. Afterward I wanted only to die. . . . But the witchcraft in me held me alive on a thread." He paused. Then: "I think I can never, ever, attempt that again, alone."

Bet said quickly, "But you'll never need to. I shall be here." She had wanted to comfort him, and he raised his tired head toward her in acknowledgment.

She said, "Do you think—well, would it be possible perhaps to make me even a little smaller? Nearer to the size I used to be."

The mole became almost brisk. "Of course. Together we should be able to manage *that*. But we must be careful to adjust accurately."

The mole came out of his tunnel, and Bet got to her feet and then stooped and touched him. Together, very carefully, with many stops and starts, they willed shrinkage, until at last Bet could stand up straight and say, "That's it! I'm the right size! I feel it; I know it!"

The mole was snuffling to himself, in satisfaction at a job well done.

Now that she was her comfortable self again, Bet's walk home did not seem so long. She was back in her bedroom well before her grandmother's time for getting up, and it seemed that her grandfather had not needed to thump during the night.

To Bet it hardly seemed worthwhile to take off her outdoor clothes. So she was standing by the window, fully dressed, when Mrs. Allum looked in to see how she was after yesterday's alarm. Mrs. Allum had not admitted that there was anything unusual about Bet's size, but now she paused in the doorway to stare. Then she gave a little cry of pleasure and relief: "Oh, that's my girl again!"

XVII

COME HELL OR HIGH WATER

RESTORED to her right shape and size, Bet looked back with near disbelief on the events of that hot afternoon, when aboveground, her grandmother had spring-cleaned so furiously, while Mr. Franklin was out of the way in London on his book hunt.

On that afternoon Bet had descended into the earth to the mole's secret world of cool passageways and chambers, storerooms and vaults, where no human being had ever been before—or, perhaps, would ever go again. All her life she would remember the strangeness and—at one point—the solemn fearfulness of that chthonic adventure. She thought of the mole differently now: an earth master, indeed!

However, neither of them spoke of what they had experienced together. After all, it had been intended as a test of the power of the witchcraft at the mole's command. Now they were certain that with Bet's help, he could use witchcraft to get rid of witchcraft.

When?

The mole knew that as soon as the school holidays began, Bet was going to stay with her new family. It would be an important step for her to take.

"After that, perhaps?" he suggested.

Bet, however, was asking anxiously. "While I'm away, you won't be going off to Hampton Court or anywhere? You will be here when I get back from my mum's?"

The mole said: "I shall wait here. I promise. When he was a schoolboy, Master Y had this slangy saying, 'Come hell or high water,' he'd do whatever it was. And he did. And so shall I."

"Good," said Bet. "Because, when I get back, you'll want to hear about my mum and everything. I'll be able to tell you then."

"Yes, indeed," said the mole. "And after that . . . "

"I suppose so," Bet said slowly, unwillingly, and still unwillingly, "Yes, of course."

No more was said on the subject.

Bet went on her visit as soon as the term ended. She began to feel at home with her family. She liked going out with her mother and the baby, to do the household shopping. She liked helping her mother in the flat, especially with the cooking. Her stepfather liked his food, and they all ate well. Most of all, she liked helping to bathe the baby—especially as her mother often asked Maddy if she would like to come down and help, too.

On the second night of her stay, Bet was woken by thunder and lightning and rain—torrential rain. The heat wave was suddenly over. It was succeeded—most unusually for this season of the year—by almost continuous rain. Day after day it rained as if it would never stop, and the weather forecasters warned of the danger of flooding in some parts of England.

Bet and Maddy—they were together now, most of the time—never bothered much with weather forecasts.

Then Mrs. Allum telephoned with the news that the river by the Franklin cottage had risen and was now brimming its banks, and water was welling up in the meadow in wide puddles. The old gray pony had been taken away into safety. She and Mr. Franklin were busy getting up mats and rugs from the ground floor of the cottage, and he had insisted on all his books—his own and old Miss Franklin's—being moved out of harm's way. For the present he was staying on in his upstairs bedroom.

Maddy thought it sounded exciting; Bet felt uneasy.

The next evening Mrs. Allum telephoned again. The river and the meadow were one sheet of moving water. Water had begun to enter the cottage, seeping through ancient brickwork and then, in a rush, through the doorways. Mr. Franklin had had to leave. He was now staying elsewhere with an old acquaintance.

Bet, anxious for a friend at peril, said, "Oh, I want to go back! I must go back! Please—please!"

"Gran told me to tell you not to think of any such thing," said her mother. "She's far too busy with everything that's cropped up to have you at home just now, she says. And your grandpa's being difficult again, into the bargain."

Only at the end of a full week's stay did Bet leave Disham. By now the rain had stopped at last; the floodwaters everywhere were going down or were gone.

Bet arrived home in the evening. The next morning she went with Mrs. Allum to the Franklin cottage. Mrs. Allum went inside; Bet went into the meadow.

The meadow seemed just as usual—or did it? The grass on the sodden earth sank under her every footfall, a reminder—a warning—of what so recently had been. There were still the five great trees, but no gray pony, of course, and all the molehills had been flattened or washed away.

And then she saw what was terribly wrong.

No log!

No one had noticed its going, but it had gone. The

floodwaters had swept over the meadow and around the log and nudged at it and gently heaved at it and finally dislodged it and swept it rolling away downstream with the current of the swollen river.

All that remained was a roughly oblong patch of bare earth. There was no other trace of the log or of a mole hole that had been beside it.

XVIII

Green Grow the Rushes

B ET stood where the log had lain, and she despaired. Everything was changing; things were slipping and sliding away; nothing would ever be comfortably the same again.

She tried to think calmly. Had the moles of the

meadow all drowned, trapped below ground, each in its separate tunnel system? But the mole who was her friend could not die. Was he still here—somewhere—or had the flood carried him away, like the log itself, to faraway dangers and disasters?

She wandered distractedly over the meadow, ending up by facing the only rising ground that might have escaped flooding, the wooded part on the far bank. Between the meadow and that higher piece of woodland ran the river, still full and fast with excess water.

There was just a chance.

Just supposing he were there, she must try to attract his attention. She thought of their "Tirra-lirra!" but that had been agreed on as a warning call, and she certainly did not want to warn him off—if he were there. . . .

Then she remembered the song she had sung, half to herself and half to him, while she cared for him after the death of the heron. She began at once:

I'll sing you one-O
Green grow the rushes-O.
What is your one-O?
One is one and all alone—

Then she broke off, realizing that her singing voice in the open air hardly carried across the river. She remembered Mr. Franklin's telling her to read aloud almost in a shout to begin with, so that the mole would hear and come.

She began again, this time raising her voice and singing out so loudly that even Mrs. Allum in the cottage heard and paused in her work. She was an old woman, but this was a song much, much older. She remembered her own grandmother singing it to her when she—Mrs. Allum—was a little girl.

I'll sing you two-O
Green grow the rushes-O.

What is your two-O?
Two, two the lily-white boys
Clothed all in green-O.
One is one and all alone
And evermore shall be so.

Bet thought, If only he had been able to swim, and if he were now among the trees on the far bank, and had heard her . . . surely he would recognize the song and the voice of the singer?

She sang on, closely watching the water by the far bank.

I'll sing you three-O
Green grow the rushes-O.
What is your three-O?
Three, three the rivals . . .

On the surface of the water there were all kinds of

ripples and eddies that seemed as if they must be being made by some creature moving in the river. But traced back to its beginning, the disturbance always turned out to have been started by a water weed growing up from below or, begun from above, by a willow branch low-dipping into the water. Bet went on singing.

I'll sing you four-O
Green grow the rushes-O—

Now she noticed a dark blob in the water in the shadows just under the opposite bank. Whatever it was, it was certainly progressing through the water, but not toward her at all, instead, directly upstream.

She went on singing, and watching.

I'll sing you five-O
Green grow the rushes-O—

The dark blob—whatever it was—was moving quite determinedly upstream, but all the time the current bore down upon it, so that its course was deflected. It was being carried sideways across the river, and downstream, and she saw that, inevitably, it would be carried to her side of the river, to the very spot on the bank where she stood.

She stopped singing.

She held her breath.

The dark blob reached her riverbank. There was a flurry in the water, and something small and very wet and dark began clambering up the bank. For a moment she was not even sure that this was the mole. Then she was. She was so relieved she felt almost like crying. She said, "I thought I might never see you again."

"A possibility," the mole admitted. He was still getting his breath back after the river crossing. "Yes, touch and go. Such a volume of water coming down! But you should have remembered that a mole has forewarnings through the earth. I was not entirely unprepared."

"And I didn't know that a mole could swim," said Bet.

"You have forgotten, as I have not, all those Scottish lochs less than three hundred years ago."

Bet said, "What about the other moles from this meadow?"

"Similarly saved, and now no doubt battling among themselves for tunneling space in the new territory." The mole dismissed them from the conversation. "Tell me, what of Franklin?"

"Mr. Franklin had to move out."

"And the cat, Moon?"

"Left early, to avoid drowning."

"Pity," said the mole.

Bet said, "Are you going to move back into the meadow, now the flood's over?"

"My dear child," said the mole, "the flooding may be

over, but all my tunnels will be waterlogged, and some will have collapsed entirely."

"What will you do?"

"In due course I shall set to. I must tunnel and repair, tunnel and repair. I still have all the strength and skill of a mole, in spite of any harm that witchcraft does me. Which brings me to this present moment. You are back, and I am here, and you are going to tell me—briefly—about your visit to your family. How was it?"

"Good," said Bet. She was too frightened to say more; she could see how this conversation would end.

"And your mother?"

"Mum's lovely," said Bet. "We really get on. Really."

"Good," said the mole. "Nothing more?"

"There's lots," said Bet. "But really—no, nothing more."

"Then," said the mole, "we can move on at once to the next thing, the ridding me of the last of the witchcraft."

Here was the moment that Bet had been dreading. She said, "There's nowhere to sit now. The log's gone. The earth is soggy wet."

The mole said, "There is no need to *sit* for the work we have in mind."

Bet said, "I don't think I can do it. Not today."

"When, then?"

"Later."

"Later?"

"I've only just got back from my mum's. I need a bit of a rest. After that, perhaps."

"After that, perhaps . . . " He repeated Bet's words wonderingly. Then he said, "Your mind is dark to me."

He said no more, and Bet did not answer him. She knew what she ought to say, what she ought to do. She could not. The mole's own heartfelt desire made no difference. She could not—she *could* not—give up his friendship.

Bet took a sudden, secret decision, blindly.

"About getting rid of the witchcraft," she said, "I don't think it'll work, but if you like, I'll try with you now."

"Now?"

"Yes, now."

"You have changed your mind," said the mole. "And why should our process not work? It did before, when we shrank you to mole size." Bet said nothing. The mole went on: "You know what I shall be wishing and willing, and when you touch me, you must be wishing and willing the same thing. You're ready?"

Bet heard herself say flatly, "Yes." She bent toward him.

The mole's compact little body seemed to draw itself in even more compactly with the inward-working tension of his will. His head and shoulders lifted themselves toward Bet; she stretched out her hand, fingers extended, and touched him. For a few seconds they were in contact; then the mole gave a little cry of bafflement and disappointment and fell back.

"What happened?" asked Bet, but she knew.

"Nothing," said the mole. "Nothing. I cannot understand it. Nothing at all."

They did not discuss or speculate; the mole was too bewildered, and Bet seemed to be in a hurry. Talking rather quickly, she said that she must be getting back into the cottage to help her grandmother with all the work that needed to be done after the floods. Putting everything to rights would take days and days, she said. Indeed, there might be no time at all for her to come into the meadow before visiting her family again.

Perhaps the mole was listening to all she said; perhaps he was thinking of other things. Bet could not be sure.

He said, "I shall be in the pasture whenever you return. My exact whereabouts will depend partly on how quickly the ground here dries out and becomes suitable for digging. It will also depend partly on—well, other things. But anyway, as soon as possible I mean to reopen the exit shaft by the ash tree. You remember?"

"Yes, of course, but—"

"That will at least provide me with a temporary bolt-hole, a halfway house, so to speak. You can look for me there when you come. Then, if you choose, only if you so choose, we can try again."

"No," said Bet. "Because it would be no use."

"I don't agree," the mole said steadily. "We have been friends, and friends can always help friends. You are a friend I have trusted. If you choose, you can help me to free myself from witchcraft, restore me to the true mole nature that I should have. If you choose."

Bet said desperately, "But suppose I simply can't?"

The mole said, "Think over all that I have said, and take heart, child."

With that they parted.

XIX
A PRIVATE INTENTION

M R. FRANKLIN looked out of his window over the pasture and decided to take a stroll on the riverbank in the sunshine. The day was entirely his: Sunday; no Mrs. Allum.

He was living in the cottage again after the flooding.

Moon had joined him there. In the meadow the old gray pony had been moved back. Only the molehills had not yet reappeared. And of course, the log had gone.

As usual, there would be moorhens and ducks on the river. No heron, but surely one day another would come. And this morning, if he were very lucky, he might see—as he never had, so far—a kingfisher. Mr. Franklin slung his binoculars around his neck and shut the study door on Moon, asleep on his chair. Then he set out from the cottage.

He was nearly on the riverbank and was already level with the ash tree when he noticed a new molehill, after all, and not far from it, a hole, and—"The mole!" Mr. Franklin whispered to himself.

The upper part of the mole's body was just visible in the mouth of the hole. It turned toward Mr. Franklin, as he advanced, and the mole's nose and the whiskery hairs around it twitched slightly.

This was the first time, Mr. Franklin realized, that they had seen each other—if *seen* was an allowable word—since before his accident on the ladder. He raised his voice to call out with much cheerfulness, "A lovely morning, sir!"

"Franklin?"

"The same."

"I hope," said the mole, "that you are not come with queries and theories and so-called good advice. I may be short of conversation nowadays, but to that kind I would prefer silence."

Mr. Franklin said humbly that he would feel privileged to talk with the mole on any subject of mutual interest. So first of all they talked of the weather and the effects of the recent floods. Then they spoke of Bet. By now she had paid several visits to her new family.

The mole said, "I have talked with her only infrequently since her settling in this new place, but I believe she is happy with her family and this friend she speaks of."

"The girl Maddy," said Mr. Franklin. "Yes, very happy, I think."

"Although she tells me that her mother sometimes scolds her."

"Not more sharply than her grandmother used to, but about different things, no doubt."

"And she will be going to a new school, it seems. How will she like that?"

"Bet can certainly stand up for herself," said Mr. Franklin, "and she is resourceful. Moreover, she'll be there with her friend, I gather."

"So, all in all," said the mole, "you think she is likely to be happy?"

"I think so," said Mr. Franklin. "So does Bet's grandmother, and she should know."

"I'm glad for her," said the mole. "Truly glad." He sighed.

"And yourself?" asked Mr. Franklin. "You're moving back into the meadow, I see. I'm afraid you'll have a good deal of work to do underground. But you've made a start."

"I have made for myself what one might call a temporary refuge of tunneling. It is not my intention to do more. I shall be setting off on my travels again so soon. But that is only between ourselves, please."

Mr. Franklin wanted to ask whether the mole's "travels" would take him to Hampton Court, but he did not quite dare to mention that name. So they spoke of other things, such as earthworms.

In parting, Mr. Franklin pointed out that the mole could meet Bet's friend, Maddy, when they came down together at half-term for the day. And before that Bet would be coming by herself on a visit.

"Ah," said the mole.

Later, when Bet came to the meadow, she was full of

stories of her new life, of going to parks and playgrounds with Maddy and wandering around the marketplace with her on Market Day. "You can buy anything there— *anything!*" she told the mole. And Disham was not far from the coast, so one weekend Bet's stepfather had driven all his family to the seaside for the day. Maddy had come, too. "And when the baby's old enough, we might all go on a holiday in France. And if we do, we might drive through the Channel Tunnel from England to France. Just think, a tunnel *under the sea*. You would love it."

The mole said, "You really think so?"

"Well, perhaps not. . . . "

On this visit, as before, Bet did most of the talking; the mole listened. He asked no questions. He raised no topic outside whatever Bet wished to talk about. Nothing awkward from the past was mentioned.

Bet returned to the cottage rather pleased with herself.

Mrs. Allum was getting ready to leave for home. Mr. Franklin had just paid her what he owed her for recent housework done. He saw Bet coming in from the meadow. "So you found the mole and talked?"

"Yes," said Bet, "about all sorts of things. And hasn't he done a lot of digging underground since the flood! Now there are new molehills all over the place."

"Not his, I think," said Mr. Franklin. "They will have been the work of other moles entirely."

"None of the new molehills thrown up by him? No tunneling by him?" Bet was alarmed.

Too late Mr. Franklin saw his mistake and tried to put it right. "Unless of course, he has changed his mind. He told me that he had come to a decision, but he may well have gone back on it."

"*Come to a decision*? What decision? Why is he not rebuilding his tunnels? What's going on?"

"Now, now!" Mrs. Allum said, beginning to pay

attention as Bet raised her voice, and Mr. Franklin began: "I can't tell you more than I already have, for reasons I cannot go into——"

"Then, if you won't tell me, I'll ask the mole! He'll tell me the truth." And with that Bet was out of the cottage and across the meadow toward the ash tree.

"That creature!" said Mrs. Allum, exasperated, for she was impatient to be off.

But Mr. Franklin took the matter more seriously. "Trouble," he said. "Bad trouble, I fear."

XX

MISS Z

WHEN Bet reached the ash tree, there was no sign of the mole. She knelt and put her mouth close to the mole hole and shouted down, "Hello there!"

Silence from below; then a slight noise of movement and then the mole's voice, cross: "Who calls so rudely?"

"It's only me again—Bet!" Her voice had suddenly softened. "Please come out and talk to me—please! Oh, I can't bear it!"

The mole appeared and crept out of his hole. "Whatever is the matter?"

"You're leaving here, aren't you? You're going away, aren't you?"

A short silence. Then, "Yes," said the mole.

"But why can't you stay? Why?"

The mole said, "This pleasant pasture has become like a prison to me, an iron cage. I must escape. I must move on."

Bet said, "Really, it's because of me, isn't it?"

The mole made no answer.

Bet said, "It's because I couldn't help you get rid of the witchcraft, isn't it? And it's worse than you think, because I *could* have helped you, and I deliberately didn't. And it's even worse than that, because I willed the witchcraft in you *not* to go. Did you know that?"

The mole said nothing.

"I think you did, in the end. In the end, you knew I was a friend you couldn't trust."

"My dear child," said the mole, "all living creatures are as they are. Human beings in particular—" He paused there, clearly searching for words that would not be too wounding for his listener. "Human beings are a species with natures more—more *variable* than the nature of a mole."

"You mean, they change? They betray? But I needn't have been like that. I needn't be like that now. It's not too late. I can change back. I can help you, and I will. Now. I will."

"Oh, wait!" said the mole. "Think—think carefully for a moment! Remember! If we try again, and if we succeed where we failed before, I shall become natural mole, who fears—and therefore hates—the human being that you are. I shall not be able to help myself."

"I don't care," said Bet. "Now, at this minute, what

I want most in the world is for you to be mole, wholly mole, nothing but mole. Because that's what you want, that's what you *need*, and you can trust me, your friend, to help you get that."

He had to believe her. "Very well," said the mole.

For the last time they were friends together, determined between them to achieve something heroic in the name of friendship.

Again the mole compacted his body, and again Bet reached out and touched him with a finger and let her finger remain where it touched. This time something like an electric current seemed to run between the two of them, and Bet became aware of changes and transformations even more wonderful than big to little, or little to big. First, and reluctantly, an ancient foulness, in its entirety, left the mole, and then his whole body began to shimmer with joy. At his hindquarters the shimmer solidified into something that was a little taller than a matchstick and a good deal fatter than a matchstick and otherwise not very much like a matchstick at all. For this was part of the mole's own body restored to him at last, his tail.

Bet gave a cry of delight. At the same moment the mole squealed in terror and bit her finger. Then, in frantic haste, he flung himself away from her to the riverbank and headlong into the water. Bet saw him swim across, climb the opposite bank and disappear into the darkness of the trees.

Watching from the cottage, Mr. Franklin and Mrs. Allum could not, of course, hear what was said between girl and mole, nor could they be sure of what they saw. All they were aware of was some desperate happening and then Bet's own movements. She went to sit on the very edge of the riverbank, drew her knees up under her chin, and fixed her gaze on the obscurity of the woodland opposite.

"She must come back!" fussed Mrs. Allum. "We have to get home. He'll want his tea."

Mr. Franklin said, "You can't disturb her now. She's too upset. Wait."

Mrs. Allum went to wait in the car, ready to set off at once. Meanwhile, Bet had got to her feet, turned from the river, and was coming back across the meadow. Mr. Franklin met her at the field gate. She said, "The mole bit my hand." When Mr. Franklin exclaimed in astonishment and indignation, she said, "No, it wasn't like that at all." She explained enough of the circumstance to enlighten him.

Mr. Franklin said, "I'm so very sorry—"

"No," said Bet. "I did what I most wanted to do, and it's all all right." But her voice was dreary.

Mr. Franklin tried to comfort here. "You have been a true friend to the mole, one of the best. Not Miss X or Master Y was a trustier friend than you have been."

Bet did not answer him, and Mrs. Allum was sounding the horn for her to hurry.

Mr. Franklin said, "I'm afraid you'll never want to visit here again."

"I have to come at half term," said Bet. "I promised Maddy that we'd come together then." She went on to the car, where her grandmother had already started the engine.

Weeks later, at half term, the two girls came.

Mr. Franklin was surprised by Bet's friend, Maddy. She was bouncy, rather talkative, and unabashed in company. Not in the least like Bet, but perhaps it was just because of those differences, Mr. Franklin reflected, that they got on so well.

After they had all greeted Mr. Franklin, Mrs. Allum started on her housework and Bet went into the meadow, but Maddy lingered in the cottage. Its oddity fascinated her. In Mr. Franklin's study she saw Moon asleep.

She said, "That's a lovely cat. So white."

"It's called Moon," said Mr. Franklin.

"That's right," said Maddy.

"Right?"

"I mean, his name suits his color, doesn't it?"

Mr. Franklin watched Maddy. Now she was examining the books still piled on tables and chairs, waiting to be reshelved. She was chatting to herself as she puzzled out some of the titles. She picked on one of the thickest volumes. "*Alfred Lord Tennyson*—that's poetry, isn't it, Mr. Franklin?"

"Yes, it is."

Maddy held the book in both hands, murmuring, "My! It really is heavy!"

Mr. Franklin looked curiously at Maddy. Probably she knew all that he knew of the happenings in the meadow. Bet would have told her. But had Bet told her even more? There was at least one mystery he would like to have solved. (As usual, he longed to *know,* to *understand.*)

He said, "Before the recent flood here—"

He paused.

Maddy said, "Yes?"

"Before the flood here, there was a day when something odd happened in the meadow."

"Odd?" said Maddy.

"Well, it *seemed* odd. Something to do with Bet's size."

"Size?" said Maddy.

"She suddenly seemed—well, you know, *bigger.* Temporarily *bigger.* Has she ever talked to you about her size?"

"Oh, yes!" cried Maddy. "Of course, Mr. Franklin! Because Bet's a little older than I am, so it's not surprising that she's taller than I am. Bigger, you know. Was that what you meant, Mr. Franklin?"

"Not exactly," said Mr. Franklin, "but it doesn't matter."

Their eyes met; Maddy's gaze was bold, but also blank.

She was giving nothing away. Mr. Franklin realized then—and it is a useful bit of knowledge—that a talkative person can also keep secrets.

After exploring the cottage and its contents, Maddy joined Bet out in the meadow. "Where was the log that got swept away in the floods?" she asked.

The baldness where it had lain was beginning to disappear as the grass and meadow weeds grew over it. But Bet found the place, and they stood there. Maddy, gazing around, said, "Just look at the molehills!"

Bet explained about other moles in the meadow, each one living separately in its own tunnel system.

"And your mole might be one of them, Bet."

"He was never my mole; he belonged to himself always. But if he were here, we'd never know."

Maddy was not satisfied. "Look at the molehills!" she said again.

"I have."

"No, but the molehills nearest to this bare patch, nearest to where the log used to be—look! They're roughly in a circle, in a deliberate circle."

Bet turned slowly around—right around. Maddy was right. The molehills were arranged like a necklace around the very spot where the log had been, where so often she and the mole had met for reading aloud or for talk. But she said, "The mole warned me that he would have no memory of what had been."

Maddy said, "Well, I don't remember things that happened long ago when I was very little, and yet I *nearly* remember. It could be like that for him."

Bet stood on the bare patch and stared at the molehills and thought over what her friend had just said. She felt some kind of comfort creeping into her.

Maddy was going from molehill to molehill. "You must take something home with you as a memento." With her fingers she was sifting through the fine soil of each molehill in turn. "Here's quite a pretty little stone you could keep." She moved on. "Or a snail shell, but it's broken." She moved on again. "And here's an old metal button—I think. Very dirty."

Bet sprang forward. "Oh, yes, that's what I want!" She did not yet say why. They took the object indoors to the tap in the scullery and began scrubbing at it.

"Not a button," said Maddy. "Perhaps an old lucky threepenny bit?"

They scrubbed on. "Not a coin at all," said Bet, puzzled. Cleaned up, this was just a flat silvery disk with a hole punched in it, off center.

"Quite a lot of writing scratched on one side," said Maddy. "An address . . . "

"The address of this cottage!" said Bet, peering. Then she understood. "There'll be a dog's name scratched on the other side—yes! S-u-n-n-y. He was old Miss Franklin's dog, long ago—-you remember? I did tell you. This is his identity disk."

"So the mole cast it up in the waste earth of one of

his molehills. He meant it for you, Bet."

"Perhaps," said Bet.

"Truly," said Maddy, and she saw that Bet clasped the disk tightly in her hand.

Later, when they were about to go home, Bet went alone into the meadow, with the disk in her pocket, to look again at the necklace of molehills. She dared to say aloud, "I really think Maddy may be right." She smiled to herself. "Yes."

Hugging that thought to her, Bet went back to the car. Mr. Franklin was waiting to see them off. He looked anxiously at Bet. "All right?"

"Oh, yes!" She smiled at him, as she had smiled to herself in the meadow. She said, "And I would like to come again someday, please, with Maddy."

He was relieved, happy for her. He said, "Any day, my dear Miss Z."